The
Big
Mama
Stories

The Big Mama Stories

Shay Youngblood

Firebrand
Books

Ithaca, New York

Selections from this book have appeared previously in *Catalyst*, *Common Lives/Lesbian Lives*, *Conditions*, and *The Stories We Hold Secret* (Greenfield Review Press).

Several stories have been adapted for the stage in the play *Shakin' the Mess Outta Misery*, first produced by Horizon Theatre Company in Atlanta, Georgia (1988).

Copyright © 1989 by Shay Youngblood
All rights reserved.

This book may not be reproduced in whole or in part, except in the case of reviews, without permission from Firebrand Books, 141 The Commons, Ithaca, New York 14850.

Book design by Mary A. Scott
Cover design by Debra Engstrom
Cover art by Desne A. Crossley
Typesetting by Bets Ltd.

Printed in the United States on acid-free paper by McNaughton & Gunn

10   9   8   7   6   5   4   3

Library of Congress Cataloging-in-Publication Data

Youngblood, Shay.
    The big mama stories.

        Contents: Born with religion — Snuff dippers —
An independent woman — (etc.)
        1. Afro-American women—Southern States—Fiction.
2. Southern States—Fiction.   3. Women—Fiction.
I. Title.
PS3575.O8535B5   1989   813'.54   89-1315
ISBN-0-932379-58-3 (alk. paper)
ISBN 0-932379-57-5 (pbk. : alk. paper)

For all my Big Mamas—
Luellen, Jennie Mae, Mary Lee, Bessie, Lillian, Nettie Mae,
Charlie Mae, Jackie, Maxine, Myrtice, and Mineola

Acknowledgments

Thanks . . . Muchos Gracias . . . Mille Merci:
Kelley Alexander • Nancy Anderson • Henrietta Antonin •
Isabelle Bagshaw • Carolyn Bemis • Debra Brooks • Charis
Books • Cast of *Shakin' The Mess Outta Misery* • Clark College
Communications Department • Laurie Cubbin • Lorraine
Deschamps • Susan Edwards • Nikky Finney • Sabrina Freeney
• Robin Gillard • Susan Harte • Valarie Henry • Sherry Langlais
• Marlene, Brooke, and Leni • Deborah Moton • National Black
Women's Health Project Network • Mary and Marion Porter •
Rosina Riley • Sandra Robinson • Carole Rubenstein • Sisters
• Ellen Speyer • Sabrina Sojourner • Lillie Steadman • Carole
Tucker.

The French Connection:
Nancy Buell • The Chutkows • Alane Freund • Ange Guillot
• Odile Hellier • Eve Humphreys • Heidi Iratcabal • Jane et
Fernando • Ted Joans • Judith Karolyi • Anne, Natasha et Alain
Moutot • Laurence Perez • Ken Rabin • Anne Renardet •
Steven Vitale • Jason Weiss • for endless financial and
emotional support, love and hugs to the gypsy and writer that
I am.

Cheryl Clarke • Kay Hagan • Nicholasa Mohr • The Pamoja
Writer's Group and Toni Cade Bambara • Barbara Smith • for

the crucial feedback on my writing and keeping me on the writing track.

American Aid Society (France) • Hambidge Center for the Creative Arts • M. Karolyi Foundation • Money for Women/ Barbara Deming Memorial Fund • Virginia Center for the Creative Arts • Yaddo • for the timely financial support of my work and in many cases a quiet place in which to find the words to tell these stories.

There are so many others whose love and encouragement I carry with me daily. Thank you.

Contents

Born With Religion

The downtown projects, where we lived then, had lines that marked us inside. Four square blocks of two-story red brick apartments. Ten units of ten apartments in each row. Ten rows to a block. Two blocks on either side of Seventh Avenue, the street that ran through the middle of the projects. The front line of apartments at the south end faced Front Street, a block-long row of shops—Fat Daddy's Rib Shack on the corner, Miss Corine's Beauty Shop next to it, Pitts Funeral Home, Mr. Johnny's Grocery Store-Liquor Shop and backroom juke joint, Mr. Wylie's TV and Radio Repair Shop, and Mr. Ben's Barbershop. Eighth Avenue ran along the west line and separated the projects from the three cemeteries.

Winston was a dusty, treeless lot where the poorest Black folks was buried (and where the juiciest blackberries growed between the plain gray headstones). A few old scary trees and bushes looking like they was from biblical times squatted among the patches of brownish-green grass in East Winston, where poor Blacks who carried insurance policies was buried. Most of the graves there sported bright plastic flowers and fresh hoe marks from where families had recently cleaned the graves. Next to East Winston, separated by a heavy chain-link fence, was the white folks' cemetery. It was left over from when whites lived downtown, long before the projects. Lime-green artificial-looking grass grew there. Families of the dead white folks put fresh wreaths and pots of flowers on the graves. There was a death house there too, where it was said that some white folks was buried standing up. Big Mama said they was probably too stubborn or mean to lay down.

Seventh Avenue bordered the east side of the projects, where a row of raggedy, wooden shotgun-style houses with dirt yards half stood, half leaned against each other. Further down, across Church Street, there was four houses—big, old Victorian ones, with pretty grass growing in they yards and flower beds in all but the boardinghouse yard where working men with no family had rooms. The gray house belonged to Mr. Pitts and Miss Rosa from the funeral home. My English teacher, Miss Georgia Butts, lived in the blue one. And Miss Lily and Miss Tom lived in the white one with the green shutters.

Church Street ran across the center of the projects on the other side of Seventh Avenue. Eighth Street Baptist Church was in the middle of that block surrounded by small brick houses built just alike. In front of the church was a glassed-in bulletin board with Reverend Waters' doctored-up quotes from the Bible, such as: "THE LORD GIVETH AND THE LORD WILL TAKETH AWAY THAT NEW BUICK IF YOU DON'T THANK HIM PROPERLY . . . PRAISE THE LORD IN HIS HOUSE."

On the north line was Highway 22. It ran east through our lil town of Princeton, Georgia, across the wide, fast, and muddy Backbend River, into the smaller country town of Prayerville, Alabama.

Me and Brother lived with Big Mama then. She was the only mama we knowed. We didn't call her Big Mama cause she was big or even cause she was our mama, cause she wasn't either. She was just regular. A old Black woman who had a gift for seeing with her heart. A brown-skinned woman. Brother, who had an eye for color, called her dark sienna. She kept her long, mixed-gray hair plait up and wrapped across the top of her head. Her face was a place where deep lines drew high cheekbones that showed the Cherokee in her, and a place where dark, knowing brown eyes showed their love for every living thing, cept maybe roaches. Her body was warm and full of soft places to lean into. In hard times folks be leaning on Big Mama. Like our blood mama, who left me and Brother with her five years ago when I was six.

The story was told to me that a slick-talking beauty supply salesman driving a yellow convertible come to call on the shop where Mama fixed hair. When he offered her a piece of the road, she dropped that greasy hot comb she was holding over some poor woman's head and they lit out of town in a cloud of fine red dust. Every now and then we'd get a postcard from her saying how she was gonna send for us soon as "they" got settled, but times were still hard up North too.

Things be going bad for Big Mama, she would up and go to the Bible. She had faith in the power of the man above to work miracles, and me, I had faith in Big Mama.

Like the time Brother got put in jail for running numbers. Big Mama was up late every night reading out loud from the Bible. She was doing some serious praying down there on her knees, eyes closed, work-wore hands pressed together, pointed toward heaven, elbows digging deep into her side of the bed. Bout three days later Brother came stepping in the back door with a plate of ribs smoking in one hand and a hat box in the other one. All he said was, "Thank you, Big Mama." She said, "Boy, you better be thanking the Lord." She was always giving credit to the Lord.

When Aunt Viola got that growth in her stomach, everybody knew she was too old to have a baby. The doctor said it was a tumor, and he was gonna have to cut her open. That was gonna be risky since she was over seventy-five years old. Well, Aunt Vi wouldn't hear bout no surgery.

"I been with an uncut belly this long, I believe I'll just keep on till the Lord takes me home." Aunt Vi had a way of keeping Jesus in every conversation. She sure was Big Mama's blood sister— them women loved the Lord.

Now Aunt Vi believed that roots and herb medicines could cure anything. After the doctor's report she went to everybody in the neighborhood she knew could heal, then went to others she heard about. A couple of weeks later she looked bout ready to deliver that tumor. Big Mama, being her closest living kin, got worried and called a special meeting of the #2 Mission Prayer Circle to pray over Aunt Vi. Come dark, and just shadows apart, five elder sisters of the church eased in the back door. They would make their way through the kitchen to the front room, crowded with heavy, out-dated furniture. Pictures of children Big Mama had raised covered the walls in frames of their own or stuck inside frames of the lifelike portraits of Jesus or the gold framed double portraits of Dr. King and President Kennedy. Chairs were arranged in a raggedy circle. Aunt Vi was leaned back into the most comfortable chair, waving a funeral fan to knock flies from her swollen legs.

Aunt Mae, Big Mama's other sister, didn't come cause she said she wasn't member of no church and besides she always went to the dog races over in Alabama on Tuesday nights. Said she would pray where she wanted to, but she would pray.

Miss Mary always showed up first. She looked like a skinny black gypsy. She had six gold teeth right in front, wore big gold earrings and bright-colored scarves over her finger-length plaits that stuck out from under. Then come Miss Alice, a light-skinned sister with the bluest eyes and hair I'd ever seen. Then Miss Tom come in. She was a mannish-looking woman with a mustache. She took the neighborhood kids fishing every summer. Then Miss Emma Lou come in, short, dark, and bowlegged, still wearing her white maid's uniform and carrying that spit cup. The woman didn't go nowhere without a tin of sweet Georgia Peach snuff in her apron pocket and a old tin can that she kept under every chair and pew she took up space on. And late, as always, come Miss Lamama. Her real name was Jessie Pearl Lumumba. At seventeen she married a African and took to wearing African dresses and took on African-like ways.

I got sent upstairs so the grown folks could meet, but I only went up halfway so I wouldn't miss nothing. There was a call to order to set old business straight and get on with the new. Miss Alice reported on her visits to the sick members of the congregation. "Sister English is recuperating in satisfactory condition from her gallbladder operation, and she preciates the chewing tobacco and peppermint candies that we took up collection to buy for her. Brother Solomon's cataract operation was a success. He says it's scandalous, though, how short them nurses are wearing their uniforms. He's seeing more now than he ever wanted to."

Then Miss Mary read a long passage from the Bible. St. Matthew, 9th chapter, verses 1 through 27. It was bout how Jesus cured the sick, raised the dead, and healed the blind. Miss Mary got to reading loud in the end like she was bout ready to start shouting. . . . *then the almighty Jesus said, 'daughter be of good comfort; thy faith has made thee whole.' Hallelujah!* I couldn't hardly hear after that for the hand clapping, foot stomping, and *amens* that rocked the front room.

A low humming started round the edges of the room. The uneven sound of them old women calling on the spirit to move in them mysterious ways. It caught me by surprise and held me still. When I peeped round the corner of the stairwall, I saw Aunt Vi in the center of the circle moaning and singing and rocking back and forth. She started to testify bout how she had been afflicted for months with a tumor and a doctor, both who had given her nothing but misery. *Lord-Jesus-Mother Mary, bless this tired old body. I know you won't gimme more than I can bear, Jesus. I just ask that this load of mine be lightened so I can continue to do God's work more better.* The sisters shook they heads in agreement and threw they right hands in the air to testify to her speaking the truth. When Aunt Vi finished her prayer, everybody shook her right hand. Miss Lamama in African tradition kissed her on both cheeks.

Then Big Mama let out a song, souls deep. *Precious Lord, take my hand.* . . . Made my knees shake. A chill went through me and I got hot, all at the same time. Right then something happened to me. Felt like I was falling back up inside myself. Felt funny, and tingly, like I might've been hit by a streak of lightning. My body started swaying, and all I could think bout or hear was the sound of Big Mama singing that song. When the song was over I came back to myself. Some of the sisters was crying and blowing they noses. Looking at Big Mama, nobody could tell just how much power she had over people. I promised myself from then on to do everything she said quick, before she spoke twice.

She could move people. They didn't know it was Big Mama making folks feel the spirit, and all that time folks giving credit to God.

Big Mama said a closing prayer for the health and strength of all God's children. Then the meeting was adjourned, and the women started crowding round to touch or lay hands on Aunt Vi in the center of the circle.

I almost fell down the stairs when Big Mama called me. "Chile, come on in here and pour the ladies some tea." I thought she had seen me through the wall. There was iced tea, sugar cookies, and my favorite, chicken salad on white bread. And there was some peach brandy Big Mama made out of peach peelings and plenty of sugar and water. She kept it in a covered jar in the pantry next to the water heater. The ladies started catching up on other folks' business, home remedies, and family problems. Just like Miss Mary always came first and Miss Lamama always came late, Miss Alice was always having troubles with her husband, Mister Henry. One day the week before she came home to find her antique upright piano was missing. Come to find out Mister Henry had pawned it along with the breakfast dishes to pay off his gambling debts. Big Mama shook her head in disgust, told Miss Alice to have faith and pray over her troubles. "Either the Lord will make a way or you gonna have to put a lock on the kitchen sink, Alice."

"Or a knock upside his head," said Miss Emma Lou, taking aim at her old tin cup. "Now that'll fix him."

Even Miss Tom who didn't spare words had to add, "A man is only good for a few things, and if he can't do them right you don't need him. You can do poorly by yourself."

As usual Miss Alice started making up for all of Mister Henry's faults by saying he was a sick man, and as usual nobody paid her no mind. If she hadn't been taking up for him all the time, Big Mama might've fixed him.

It was almost midnight when everybody left, but Big Mama didn't stop. She was up for hours praying over Aunt Vi's tumor. I watched her lips moving by the light of the big white candle my blood mama sent us Christmas last. She took a big breath and look right up in my eyes like she knowed I'd been studying her all the time.

"Chile, why you ain't sleep yet?"

"Cause I was thinking."

"What you thinking so hard bout?"

"Bout dying."

"You too young to be thinking bout dying, sugar."

She blew out the candle and got up in the bed next to me. My head found a warm soft spot on her chest that smelled a lil bit like peach brandy.

"Not me, Big Mama. I'm scared you might die, then what I do?" My eyes filled up and my throat got tight saying it out loud.

"Who said I'm going anywhere? You my sugarfoot. I wouldn't leave you for all the angels in heaven."

"What if you got sick like Aunt Vi and . . . ."

"When the last time you knowed me to be sick? Listen baby, your Big Mama got a whole lot more living to do. I ain't going nowhere till the Lord is ready for me. Stop worrying unnecessary and go on to sleep. You got too many Big Mamas to be worrying bout all that. Have sweet dreams, baby. I want you to have sweet dreams."

She hugged me up close to her and hummed a lil song. Finally I did go to sleep, with the smell of burning candles on the air and pictures of Big Mama laughing at death in my head.

The sisters of the #2 Mission Prayer Circle kept coming to our living room every Tuesday night to testify, sing, preach, and pray over Aunt Vi. In the middle of one meeting, Aunt Vi fell out. She tipped over backward on the floor holding on to her tumor. I started crying cause I knew she was dead. Miss Alice, who had some nurses' training, said to be calm. Big Mama told me to hush. She took up Aunt Vi's hands and closed her eyes for a minute. Then she run a open bottle of green camphor oil with cotton balls in it under Aunt Vi's nose. It brought her back to life. Big Mama be dealing serious. After that night I never worried much bout losing Big Mama to death. She had too much power to go anywhere she didn't want to, and I knew she never wanted to leave me.

Slowly but surely Aunt Vi's stomach went down to its normal layered look. Eight weeks to the day after the first prayer meeting was called, she reported that her tumor had disappeared.

"That doctor said it was a miracle, but I told him it was the prayers of the faithful and the will of God that made me well," she said.

But me, I knew it was Big Mama again, shaking the mess out of misery.

Snuff Dippers

I have always had a deep and undying respect for the wisdom of snuff dippers. Big Mama raised me in the company of wise old Black women like herself who had managed to survive some dangerous and terrible times and live to tell bout them. These were hard-working, honest women whose only admitted vice, aside from exchanging a lil bit of no-harm-done gossip now and then, was dipping snuff.

Big Mama and her friends was always sending me to Joe's grocery store on the corner to buy silver tins of the fine brown powder wrapped in labels with names like Bruton's Sweet Snuff, Georgia Peach, and Three Brown Monkeys. The summer I was six my mean older cousin, DeeDee, told me that snuff was really ground up monkey dust, a delicacy in the royal palaces of Africa. She told me to mix three heaping tablespoons of snuff with a glass of milk and to drink it through a straw fast like a chocolate milkshake.

"If you drink it all," she said, shaking her nine-year-old hips, "you'll wake up and be real pretty like them African dancing girls we saw on TV. They drink it every day. It'll make your teeth white too."

"How come you know so much?" I asked suspiciously.

"Cause when I went to New York to see Aunt Louise she lived next door to a African dancing girl. She told me herself that's how come she was so pretty."

DeeDee was so convincing, especially when she made me promise on the Bible not to tell nobody.

I took one of Big Mama's good glasses with flowers painted on it down from the top shelf of the china cabinet. Then I mixed the milk and monkey dust, stirring it in the pretty glass till it made me sneeze. Holding my nose, I stuck a plastic straw into the foaming brown stuff and began to drink my way to beauty. Big Mama heard me coughing and crying and come in the kitchen. When she found out what I was doing she shook her head and tried not to laugh at me. She gave me some baking soda to rinse my mouth out and a lecture on not believing everything I heard. Said I was already pretty, and all the monkey dust in the world couldn't give me a good, kind, honest heart. I never forgave DeeDee for that trick. I was dizzy for hours, and the taste of the nasty, bittersweet snuff lingered on my tongue long after the humiliation had gone.

When I was a few years wiser and had the nerve to question Big Mama, I asked her why she dipped snuff. Big Mama leaned back, deep into her rocking chair. She slowly drew a fresh tin of snuff from her apron pocket. After opening the can, she took a big pinch of the brown stuff between her index and forefinger like I'd seen her do a million times. With her other hand she stretched out her bottom lip to take in the dip of snuff. She slapped her hands together and wiped them on her apron before she answered me. By the way she took her time I knew she was gonna tell me a story. Big Mama started out by defending herself.

"Snuff ain't no worse than them cancer sticks that be killing folks left and right. I ain't never heard tell of snuff harming nobody. But as I recollect, back in '57 when the only place colored folks could sit on a bus was in the back, Emma Lou came close to getting us killed on the #99."

Big Mama told me that over twenty years ago the #99 bus was known as the "maids' bus." It arrived downtown at the corner of Broadway and 12th Streets every weekday morning at 6:00 A.M. to pick up the Black domestic workers bound for the rich white suburb of Northend, ninety minutes away. The sun would just be creeping up behind the glass and steel office buildings to light the women's way. From a distance, the #99 bus stop looked like any other corner where buses stopped. Bout forty Black women stood there dressed as if on their way to a church social. They all carried shopping bags made of plastic, paper, or straw, advertising the names of places they would never see or stores where they weren't welcome. In the bags were maids' uniforms that pride prevented them from wearing outside the places where they worked in them.

Everybody had a regular seat on the #99 so that friends and neighbors could sit together recreating communities. Miss Emma Lou sat in the seventh row, right-hand side next to the window, and Miss Mary sat next to her. Seats weren't assigned, but all hell cut loose when the pattern was broken by a newcomer. Newcomers sat up front—period.

Big Mama said that conversations on the #99 went something like this.

Miss Emma Lou: "My lady asked me to come in on a Sunday afternoon, would you believe, to pour tea for some English foreigners visiting her mama. I told her that her mama was gonna have to pour that tea herself cause I had to go to church on Sunday. The Lord wouldn't preciate my missing a prayer service to pour tea for the Queen of England."

Miss Mary: "My white lady, bless her heart, is as simple as a chile. When the boss was near bout fifty years old he turn round and left the other missus and two grown children to marry this girl right out of college. This chile, believe me when I tell you, sends her drawers to the dry cleaners. Ain't that nothin? A woman that cain't wash her own drawers."

Miss Mary and Miss Emma Lou lived in one-bedroom apartments on either side of me and Big Mama in the housing projects by the river. Miss Mary was a tall, straight-backed, thin Black woman, somewhere in her sixties, who looked like a gypsy. She wore big gold earrings and bright-colored head ties that matched her dresses. Sometimes in the middle of a conversation with her Miss Mary would see into your future and start to tell it if you didn't stop her. Folks said she come from a line of West Indian root women, seers and healers, and couldn't help it. Miss Emma Lou tried to convince her to charge for the privilege of knowing people's future, but Miss Mary said that would be highway robbery, charging money for a gift give to her by God.

Miss Emma Lou was Miss Mary's best friend. She was a short, heavyset brown-skin woman who was as bowlegged as Miss Mary was straight in the back. Unlike the other maids, Miss Emma Lou wore her white uniform most of the time—said it was the mark of a professional. She made her white folks refer to her as a domestic engineer and got paid a lil bit extra for it. Miss Emma Lou wasn't nobody's fool. And she was a snuff-dipping woman who said what was on her mind and emphasized her point by spitting snuff juice in a can she carried with her everywhere.

Then there was Ralph, a big, red-faced Irishman with laughing green eyes and curly blond hair, who had been the driver for the #99 since the service began in 1952. Dr. J. R. Whittenhauser, the millionaire doctor, had stopped Ralph's gypsy cab on Peachtree Street and offered him an easier job with a steadier income. All he had to do was pick up the domestic help for Northend by 6:00 A.M. Monday through Friday and pick them up again at 3:30 P.M. in a bus Northend residents bought for that purpose. Even if the city buses went on strike or riots broke out, white ladies in Northend would have their meals cooked, children looked after, and laundry done.

Ralph was one of the nicest white men she ever met, according to Big Mama. If one of the regular riders was late, Ralph would wait a few more minutes knowing that on Fridays Miss Lamama had to walk her grandchildren to school and on Mondays Miss Mary did a sunrise ritual. If it was raining real hard or the temperature was real cold, Ralph would drive some of the older women with arthritis, bursitis, and bad knees across town right up to their door. In return the women baked him cakes, brought him lunch, and treated him like one of them.

Big Mama said Ralph was like one of them cause white folks treated him the same as if he was colored cause he was a foreigner. She said he even stood up to a white man for them.

Big Mama's face got real serious when she started telling me one of her stories bout the not-so-long-ago days.

"As I seem to recall, it was a scorching hot day in the middle of July when Emma Lou liketa got in a whole heap of trouble over some snuff and Ralph stood up for us like a soldier," Big Mama said.

"Not only was the weather hot, but colored folks was stirred up over the lynchings and killings of colored mens all over the South by evil white men. The whites was getting meaner as the summer got hotter. A colored woman had just been found dead. She was raped and sawed open by six white men who made her brother watch em ravish her. Some awful bloody things happened that summer." Big Mama closed her eyes and drew herself up like a chill had passed over her.

"What happened, Big Mama?" I asked impatiently, as children do.

"Hold on, chile, I'm getting to it. A story ain't something you just read off like ingredients on a soap box. A story's like a map— you follow the lines and they'll take you somewhere. There's a way to do anything, and with a story you take your time." She shook a finger in my direction.

"I'm sorry, Big Mama." I was afraid I'd messed up and she wouldn't finish the story. I promised to hush and not interrupt her again.

Big Mama shifted herself into a more comfortable position for storytelling and cocked her head back for better memory.

"As I was bout to say, the #99 was rolling toward town. Most of the women on the bus was talking bout how hot it was. Breakfast milk spoiling on the table, clothes drying stiff on the line quick as lightning strike, and lil babies crying all day long they was so miserable. We was all real hot, sweaty, and wore out. Emma Lou was sitting in her regular seat by the window, Mary was next to her, and I was sitting behind them at my window seat.

"I was sitting there listening to Emma Lou go on bout how her white folks was going on a vacation in Europe, or somewhere like that, and just looking out the window. We was still in Northend, where most of the rich white folks live, and I took notice of this brand new white convertible Cadillac cruising long side of the bus. It was a white man and woman in the car. She had on a pretty white dress and looked just as brown as your Cousin DeeDee, but she had long yellow hair that was blowing all round her face. The white man was driving. He had yellow hair too, but he was real red; his skin was peeling off him like a boiled toma-to. Look like he'd been to Florida and stayed in the sun too long. He had on a pair of them mirror sunglasses so you couldn't see his eyes like them small-town redneck sheriffs useta wear to scare coloreds. You can tell a whole heap bout a person by look-ing in they eyes. You can just bout see what's going on in they mind, and some people have some terrible things on they mind."

Big Mama stopped talking again, but I didn't say nothing, and in a minute or two she kept on.

"Well, you know Emma Lou got to have her a dip of snuff. Don't care where she is or who she with, she gonna have her a taste. That day wasn't no different, but that day Emma Lou didn't have her spit cup with her. She probably left it at her white lady's house. She asked Lamama if she could use her fancy Ethiopian handkerchief, but Lamama was offended. Told her to use her bag, but Emma Lou had her white folks' lace tablecloths in there. Wouldn't you know it, just as them white folks in they brand new Cadillac was passing the bus, Emma Lou stuck her head out the window and let out a long stream of thick, brown snuff spit right in that white woman's face and on her pretty white dress.

"When the other womens on the bus saw what had hap-pened, they started falling off they seats they was laughing so hard. Ralph hear what happen and he laugh too, but pretty soon we all realize they wasn't nothing to laugh at. Them white folks drove up side the bus cussing and carrying on like I never heard and hope not to hear no more. All that white man could see was blood. Ralph got hold of the situation and threw the bus in high gear. That Cadillac speeded up too. Folks on the bus got quiet. All we could hear was the bus tires hitting the road and that raging white man calling us every kind of nigger he could think of. Ralph say, 'I'm trying to get rid of this fool. Hang on ladies.'

"For a few minutes we thought Ralph had lost them, but be-fore we got out of Northend a police car with flashing blue lights and a crying siren signaled for the bus to pull over. Ralph start-ed cussing like a sailor, but he had to pull over for the law. Out of the corner of my eye I saw the colored Catholic woman from up North cross herself. I started praying myself cause I saw the white Cadillac pull up and park behind the police car.

"The white woman jumped outta that car looking ugly like somebody called her mama nigger. She had wiped most of the spit off her face, but she still had brown snuff stains on the front of her dress. The white man had evil and ugly wrote all over him. He was hollering at the policeman and waving his fist round. The police officer, a blond-headed boy with cold blue eyes, had to hold him back from getting on the bus. The policeman got on though and look us over like we stole something. He say out loud, 'Which one of you aunties spit on Mr. Roger's friend?' As if we was children and any one of us could've been his mama, grandma, or help raise him.

"Nobody made a sound. Then he put his hand on his hip by his gun and say real nasty, 'I'm gonna have to lock every one of y'all up if don't nobody speak up right now.' We didn't hardly breathe. When he ask Ralph who spit on the white lady, Ralph say, 'Might be a pigeon thought he was flying over the ocean and took a notion to shit in the sea. Why you want to bother these nice ladies?' That made the police mad. He say, 'They a bunch of niggers and one of em spit on a white lady. I don't know where you from, but we don't tolerate disrespect from our niggers here in Georgia, or from nigger-loving foreigners.'

"When Ralph stood up in front of that policeman you could see the blood rush to his face. He was mad as all git out. The policeman back off the bus with his hand on his gun. He say loud, looking hard at Ralph, 'I want all you niggers to get off the bus. That mean everybody.' Ralph was the first one to get off the bus. Then we all got off and the policeman made us line up by the road in that hot sun like he was gonna let that crazy white man shoot us. Cars was passing long the highway with folks looking at us like we was from the moon. Then the policeman just left us standing there and went over to his patrol car and started talking on his radio.

"Before we knowed anything, that crazy white man was hollering at us, 'Somebody's gonna pay for this.' The white woman was leaning on the Cadillac looking hateful and mean as a snake. Then that fool white man started picking up rocks and dirt and throwing em at us. Mary still got a scar where one of them rocks split her knee. Ralph rush over to stop him, but the white man throwed dirt in his eyes. We all run screaming and hollering behind us into a patch of weeds and up against a fence a lil piece from the road till we couldn't go no further. I thought for sure we was gonna be killed. Finally the policeman see what was happening and pull the white man to the side. They look over at us standing in them knee-high weeds and briars and laughed at something that was said between em. Do you know that no-good policeman watch that crazy white man come over to where we was backed up against the fence like dogs and hark spit on each one of us. Lamama wiped our faces with her fancy handkerchief, weeping like a widow. Then the white man laughed and got in his Cadillac with his woman.

"Mary was behind me calling on her West Indian spirits and making signs. That white man pulled onto the highway, his tires kicking up dust every which way, right in the path of a tractor-trailer truck. I'll never forget it as long as I live. The sight of that big, brand new white Cadillac being knocked in the side and the surprise on them white folks' faces. It was a mess of twisted steel and burning white flesh. Mary was smiling. She crossed herself and said, 'Thank you, Jesus. Thank you, Ogun.'

"Emma Lou turned to me and said, 'Ain't it a shame that folks can be so mean with the Lord watching they every move.' She clicked her tongue like she do and spit in the direction of the wreck.

"I said to her, 'Emma Lou, it be the truth. Folks act like God don't be on the case recording everything in his Book of Life.' "

Big Mama shook her head in wonder and spit in the big tin can with the yellow peach label on it, the one she kept under her chair, to let me know she was through. I went over and hugged her tight round the middle, glad she took the time to remember with me the way things useta be.

An Independent Woman

For years Mr. Otis, Big Mama's good friend Miss Louise's brother-in-law, kept Aunt Mae company on Sunday afternoons in her upstairs bedroom. She and Mr. Otis kept the door closed and the gospel singing on the radio turned up loud. Once I asked her what they be doing in her room with the door closed.

"We be taking care of grown folks' business," was all she said. Her answer shut my mouth but not my mind to thinking that it must be more than listening to the radio they be doing all evening.

After the sun settled down and darkness fell gently round Aunt Mae's house, she could be found sitting like a queen at the head of her kitchen table pouring short glasses of Southern Comfort whiskey for women Big Mama said were loose and men she said were loud.

"That baby sister of mine, Mae Francis, always have been fast. She smart though, real independent. That woman could charm the skin off a snake," Big Mama would say.

Aunt Mae lived by herself in a big, old wooden house down the street from me and Big Mama in St. Pete's Alley, in back of the cotton mill. Before I was born, a man that was seeing Aunt Mae on the side left her the house and all but one hundred dol-

lars of his money when he died. His wife had passed shortly before he did, and his grown children tried to take Aunt Mae to
court over it. But they couldn't prove that he was crazy or that
she was a operator. Aunt Mae said she gave him a shoulder
to lean on, some understanding, and plenty of good whiskey.

"That ought to be worth something. A woman has got to look
out for herself. When that old man was making me promises,
I had him set em in ink at a lawyers office. I'd done heard too
many empty promises."

At a glance, Aunt Mae wasn't pretty like a movie star, but she
had a special sideways look in her eyes and a way with her
hands and hips that made her seem younger than most wom-
en in their sixties. She still kept her copper-and-silver hair parted
down the middle and waved down each side to her shoulders.
She wore her dresses short and bright. And didn't she love to
dance.

When Big Mama had to go to work at night sitting with a rich,
old white lady across the bridge in Prayerville, I was sent down
the street to spend those evenings with Aunt Mae. She taught
me some things bout being a woman.

"Don't you ever, long as grass is green, go nowhere with a man
unless you got money in your pocket. If you with a man that
don't mean you no good you can always tell him to go to the
devil and take you a taxicab or a Greyhound home," she useta
say.

Aunt Mae taught me some important things—like how to wear
a tall hat on a windy day, how to walk in high heels, and how
to dance with fat men. She knew so much bout dancing cause
when she was fifteen, she left her home in rural Lee County to
make her fortune in the nearest city. Her first job was working
as a dance hall girl. She would waltz or jitterbug round the floor
with customers for a dime a dance. Fat men, she useta say, were
the worst.

"All they ever wanna do was hug up and grind, so I useta plump
myself up with a pillow to keep em from getting too close to my
privates."

Women, she said, were her best customers. Most were middle-
aged women looking for a lil warm after losing a girlfriend. The

ladies, she said, were polite, big tippers, and almost never asked her to go home with them. The men, on the other hand, wanted to take care of her, but she was suspicious.

"They was expecting a compromise on my part that I could not make. I always have been my own woman. I was too independent to take like that without giving. Even when you get married, if that's a load you wanna bear, have your own. The wine taste sweeter and the berries have more juice when you have your own. When you've earned it. Take marriage for a instance. Now that's a job, darling. I earned my way dollar for dollar. I put up with other women, drunks, and gamblers, but the one thing I would not tolerate was a liar. I throwed Willie Pew out of his own house two days after I married him for lying to me."

"Did you let him come back Aunt Mae?"

"No m'am, but he wasn't too proud to beg. I told him to get up off his knobby knees and out of my face. I didn't want to hear that mess. Wasn't no room in my life for liars and that's all there was to it."

"What did you do when he left?"

"You mean when I put him out? I tell you, the day I left home and the day I got my divorce, it was like the Fourth of July. After the smoke cleared I felt free."

"So why you get married in the first place?" I asked.

"Why anybody would—for security. You got to understand, at that time I was sixteen years old and didn't have nothing but a few dimes from my dance hall days and a whole lotta ideas bout starting a after-hours liquor business. Willie Pew was good looking, he had money and brains enough to know I was a good woman. But his lying took something outta me. I never took him back in my heart. We took to going our own ways and soon parted. Forever after I decided to take a friend on the side when I felt a need. Usually them kind was married."

One time Aunt Mae said she run off with another woman's husband and run back two months later by herself. She said love only last till the shine wear off.

Mr. Otis was married. He drove a green-and-white taxicab every day cept Sunday, when he would show up at Aunt Mae's and give me a dime to go catch the ice-cream truck, making me promise to eat the cone outside and play on the porch till the street lights began to flicker on hours later. Then Mr. Otis would come down the stairs all happy-faced, smelling like whiskey and walking funny. Soon he would go home to Miss Tweedie.

We all went to the same church. Mr. Otis was a deacon. Aunt Mae, Big Mama, Miss Tweedie, and her sister was all in the choir together. One time I heard Big Mama and her best friend, Miss Louise, talking bout how shameless it was that Mr. Otis didn't spend his only day off with his wife. I thought bout Aunt Mae. She only got him once a week. Poor Miss Tweedie got him the other six.

One Sunday Miss Tweedie come knocking on the front door. I peeped out at her from behind the screen door wondering why she come. She was a tall, skinny woman with a stiff neck and gray hair slicked back of her head in a bun. She held her head to one side like she was listening to something way off.

"Tell your Aunt Mae that Miss Tweedie want to talk to her for a minute," she said, wiping sweat off her neck with a pocket handkerchief.

By the time this happened my best friend Jeanette had told me, most probably, what Aunt Mae and Mr. Otis be doing behind them closed doors all Sunday afternoon. I got scared. She also said Miss Alice threw a knife at her husband Mr. Henry the time she caught him in the Club Three with just his arms round another woman. I ran up the stairs two at a time and knocked hard on Aunt Mae's bedroom door.

"Aunt Mae, Miss Tweedie at the door. She want to talk to you." I could smell Mr. Otis's cigar stinking up the hallway. I wondered if Miss Tweedie could smell it too.

After some time passed Aunt Mae said, "Tell her I be right there." I ran back downstairs to deliver the message, then kneeled behind a big chair in the living room with a view of the front door. Aunt Mae took her time coming down the steps. When she got to the door she was buttoning her new pink housedress up the front. I put my head in my hands and started praying.

"What you want, Tweedie?" Aunt Mae asked her, real casual.

"Want you to know you can have him," Miss Tweedie said, wiping her neck and looking down at the bottom of the screen door.

Aunt Mae looked right at her for a minute, real surprised, then throwed back her head and laughed loud like she do when she having a good time.

"I mean it, Mae Francis. Since Otis took up with you, all I had is trouble. Folks talk. Even the pastor know where Otis be on Sunday after church. I'm through," she said, staring straight as she could back at Aunt Mae, speaking a lil louder, looking a lil higher.

"You got the wrong idea, Tweedie. I don't need a husband. I ain't got time to take care a one. What I have is a liquor business."

Miss Tweedie almost threw her neck straight up and said, "Otis ain't bought groceries in over two years. Told me his mama in Ohio needed some operations. I found out she been dead ten years. Tell him his clothes be on the front porch this evening. G'night, Mae Francis. See you in choir rehearsal." Then she turned and walked away.

Aunt Mae went back upstairs, and a few seconds later Mr. Otis run out the front door trying to catch his wife. Me and Aunt Mae watched them out the living room window, both of us laughing out loud at the sight of Mr. Otis running on drunk legs behind Miss Tweedie with his shirt tail flying in the wind. Aunt Mae poured herself a tall glass of Southern Comfort and two splashes in a dixie cup for me. We didn't say nothing, but we was both thinking bout poor Miss Tweedie.

Aunt Mae wouldn't let Mr. Otis come back no more. She told him to his face that he was a no-good, lying skunk butt and should be ashamed for having caused Miss Tweedie so much malicious misery. She and Miss Tweedie was almost friends after that.

"Women got to stick together. Men like that give me a bad name. I try to give married women a break. I don't want to be cause of no interference like that."

Aunt Mae didn't miss Mr. Otis none.

When the Sunday after-dark crowd came later that night, Aunt Mae was laughing loud, cussing, and pouring drinks like it was any other Sunday. I mixed my splash of whiskey with a can of gingerale and sat where I could see and hear everything. One of the regular ladies that came to Aunt Mae's on Sunday night, Miss Corine, was sitting next to me by the refrigerator. That night she turned to me and asked me what I wanted to be when I was grown.

"I wanna be like Aunt Mae," I said. "I wanna be independent so every day be like the Fourth of July."

Miss Corine smiled at me and said, "Amen, chile." She knew what I was talking about. She was an independent woman herself.

Did My Mama Like To Dance?

Grown folks could be so mysterious bout certain things. Big Mama, Aunt Mae, and Aunt Viola would bend my ears back bout obeying God and my elders, talk bout everybody—only in the most Christian way, of course—and everything cept my blood mama, Fannie Mae. One time I heard somebody say she died from dancing. Somebody else I heard say she died from an old wound that was too deep to heal. I was getting to be twelve and real curious bout her.

I used to not care much bout her, hardly thought bout her cept on Mother's Day when Big Mama took me and Brother to the cemetery to put flowers on her grave. I thought bout her the time I was at Jan's birthday party when Gwen Jackson told me I had no business pointing my finger cause my mama was dead. Her words give me a hurting in my heart that was worse than a belt lick on my behind. The sweet piece of chocolate cake Miss Louise cut for me tasted like dry dumplings in my throat, and my crying stained the pretty pink tablecloth. I got up from that kitchen table and run home to Big Mama who set the table for a party just for me and her.

There was a few pictures of Fannie Mae round, but the only way I could picture her was asleep at her funeral. It seemed like a dream. I was bout six the day that Brother bust in the room

I shared with Big Mama, all out of breath. I was laying across the big double bed, reading a comic book.

"Fannie Mae dead," he said, looking hurt and lost.

I almost asked him who he was talking bout before I said, "Oh." The only other thing I could think to say was, "That mean we can't go up North now?"

Brother fell on his knees and started crying.

"Please don't cry, Brother," I begged him. His crying scared me. He was older and stronger than me, and even when he got beat for doing something bad, like cussing in church, I never saw him cry. I guess he remembered Fannie Mae better than me.

At the funeral a few days later I remember sitting in the last pew in the church with Miss Corine, the beautician, on one side of me, and big, fat Aunt Viola on the other. Brother was too broke up to come. That was the first time he run away from home. The church was full. People was standing in the back of the church when chairs and pews ran out. It was hot, and there wasn't a breeze nowhere, though a whole lot of Pitts Funeral Home fans was waving hot air round. A soldierly row of lady ushers in white dresses, shoes, stockings, and white lace hankies on they heads stood in the middle aisle humming with one white-gloved hand resting over they hearts. The two male ushers was dressed in black suits. They white gloves looked like they was separated from they bodies.

The singing coming from the choir stand that day was sad. I could hear people up in the front crying and hollering. I remember being fascinated by the peculiar shine on my new black patent leather shoes and the lace ruffle on my new socks. The heat made me sleepy, so I edged up close to Aunt Vi and leaned into her softness and slept peacefully for a while. Somebody shook me awake out of a nice dream. Aunt Vi took my hand, and we started walking out of the pew. I thought we was leaving, but we was headed for the front of the church. When we got there Aunt Vi picked me up and held me over the long white casket surrounded by flowers and standing wreaths. Fannie Mae lay inside looking like she had fall asleep. She was so beautiful it made my throat hurt to look at her.

"Do you know who this is?" Aunt Vi asked me.

"It's Fannie Mae, ain't it?" I whispered.

"She in the Lord's hands now." Aunt Vi whispered back. "We don't have to worry bout her being too pretty no more. She through dancing now."

When I was a lil older and wanted someone to remember my mama to me, all the begging I could manage wouldn't move Big Mama, Aunt Vi, or Aunt Mae to talk much bout her. Every time I asked Big Mama, she would look off somewhere over my shoulder and get real misty-eyed.

"She was a beautiful chile. Cut down just as she was starting to grow. You just like her. Look like she spit you outta her mouth." Then she wouldn't say nothing for a while. Even though I would sit quiet waiting for her to go on, she never would.

When I asked Aunt Mae, who told me most everything else I wanted to know, she would almost get tongue-tied and start to cry or reach for a glass of whiskey to calm her down.

"Don't start me to crying, baby. Your mama is dead and buried, don't raise her up to haint me. Some things just ain't meant to be said out loud once they passed.

Aunt Vi would start to rocking back and forth and humming when I asked her. I decided that I needed to talk to someone outside the family. If anybody would know bout Fannie Mae's mystery and tell me, it was gonna be Miss Corine. She knew everybody's business. Cause she ran the beauty shop on Front Street, she was in a position to listen in on everybody's life—first, second, and third-hand. She was also in a position to give her opinion on a lot of things. Standing over somebody's head for two or more hours gains they full attention.

Miss Corine was nearly six-feet tall, and she'd tell anybody quick she had pure Indian blood in her. Seminole. Her mama's people was from Florida. Some of them still lived on a reservation. You could look at her red-brown skin and the long, black braid that hung down her back, high cheekbones, and clear brown eyes that slanted upward at the corners and see that. She was also quick to admit to South Carolina Geechee on her daddy's side, which is why some folks said she talked funny, ate so much rice, and the reason her fingers could braid the wind. On top of looking good, Miss Corine could put a hot curl in the shortest, nappiest of naps and untangle thick, sassy hair on a tender-headed chile without a single tear. Some called her a miracle worker.

For me, going to Miss Corine's shop first thing on a Saturday morning was better than a birthday present. Usually I hung round the shop hours after she finished with my head, helping out. I would straighten up the stacks of magazines, empty ashtrays, and collect the balls of hair that fell from ladies' heads over the course of the morning and afternoon sessions. I would collect the hair in a paper sack for later when Miss Corine would help me make braids and wigs for my dolls who all had the wrong kinda hair—all straight and obedient. At least they skin was brown like mine. Mostly though, I sat listening to Miss Corine and the other customers who Big Mama called the walking-talking-newspapers.

Miss Corine's shop was situated in a small storefront, in between Pitts Funeral Home and Fat Daddy's Rib Shack. *Miss Corine's Beauty Shop* was painted in beautiful red-and-white script on the plate glass window of the shop. A crooked hand-lettered cardboard sign was stuck in the lower left-hand corner of the window. It read: *We Curl Up & Dye.*

It was a three-chair shop built shotgun-style, long and narrow. The walls and ceiling were painted a bright pink, and the floor was covered in black-and-white squares of linoleum. One long wall was lined with six, low, red vinyl stuffed chairs with heavy chrome armrests. A couple of low tables were stacked high with outdated hair and fashion magazines, as well as *Black True Romance* and some comic books. A small black-and-white TV was kept on during business hours. It sat on a table in the front window surrounded by Miss Corine's plants. There was a mirror running the length of the other wall and a ledge underneath it where beauty and hair supplies were kept. Three black leather styling chairs that swiveled and raised to the expert touch of Miss Corine were welded into the floor.

At the back of the shop there was a big red-and-white Coke machine, and on the right was the door to the ladies room, a tiny place with a one-seater and a cracked mirror above a pink porcelain sink and another stack of magazines. A small window on the wall at the back of the shop looked on an alley that faced a red brick wall. Miss Corine had pretty pink curtains on that window. The screen door at the other end of the shop kept flies out in the summertime and invited callers year round. The shop door was always open and somebody was usually hollering in at Miss Corine.

Once inside the shop the strong scent of Sulphur 8 hair grease was like a salve to my soul. I knew I wasn't far from a good feeling. Miss Mary said Miss Corine should've been a healer cause when she laid her hands on your head you were healed of whatever laid heavy on your heart and mind. Nobody could hardly keep from telling her what was on they mind.

Big Mama sent me to Miss Corine's every second Saturday to get my hair washed, conditioned, and straightened out. Big Mama said she almost cry when she have to do my hair for school every morning, it be so thick and woolly. Said she was getting too old to tangle with my naps. This one particular Saturday I had made up my mind to ask Miss Corine bout my mama, no matter the consequence or reaction. I waited till Miss Corine had me sitting in the low-back leather chair, my head leaned back in the wash sink under the pressure of warm water, and Miss Corine's deep massaging fingers on my scalp.

"Miss Corine, how long you know my blood mama?" I asked, knowing the worst she could do was not answer me like Big Mama. But Miss Corine don't hardly hold back nothing.

"Chile, I knowed your mama before she was knee-high to a duck. She worked here in this shop for two years."

"What was she like Miss Corine?"

"Ain't your Big Mama tell you bout her?"

"No m'am, not much. They say it hurt too much to talk bout her. Sometime Aunt Mae call me by her name and start to cry."

"She right. You look just like your mama. Fannie Mae was a real pretty girl, and nice too. Even though she was high yellow she didn't have no attitude. Always had her nose in a fashion magazine. If she said it once, she said it a thousand times: 'Miss Corine, I'm going to New York and wear dresses like that and when I do my dance everybody gonna scream.' When Carlos come through here headed North, I could see the writing on the wall. . . ."

She paused a minute, then asked me, "What you want to know, baby?"

"Did my mama like to dance?"

Miss Corine didn't say nothing. She finished rinsing my hair, then wrapped my naps in a thick, white towel and led me to the styling chair. I was just bout to repeat myself when Miss Lamama, dressed in a long, orange tie-dyed dress, opened the screen door and stuck her turban-wrapped head in.

"Corine, Rosa want to know if she can borrow one of your curling irons. She dropped hers on the concrete floor and they broke in two. She's working on Sister Davis next door."

"Sister Davis had a stroke didn't she? The pressure of all them crazy children of hers finally sent her to an early grave."

"Yes, my dear. The good sister died in her sleep, and she wasn't but fifty-seven years old."

"I know Rosa will do her head justice. Give her these. She can have em, they a spare."

I was thinking that Miss Rosa probably curled my mama's hair when she died. I'd have to thank her one day cause Fannie Mae looked good. When Miss Lamama left with the curling iron, Miss Corine took up where she left off on my head and started to talk bout Fannie Mae without me pushing.

"Your mama was consumed by love. Love is what took her away from us."

"What you mean?"

"She loved dancing too strong, and that chile loved the truth. When she and Carlos left here all Fannie Mae could see was a way to dance. I was in love with something once so I knowed what it look like."

"Was she good?"

"At dancing? Hmph! She was better than good at most things she did, but that didn't have nothing to do with it. You ever look out the back window at that brick wall across the lot?"

"Yes m'am."

"Well, that brick wall is just as hard as your mama's head was then. She was stubborn. She kept forgetting she was a colored woman living in the deep and backward South, and that it was

1956. It was before integration, before equal opportunities, before civil rights demonstrations was all on the TV and in the newspapers."

"What happened in 1956?" I egged her on, excited to find out anything bout Fannie Mae.

"What happened! How old you is chile?"

"I'm almost twelve," I said, like almost twelve was grown enough to know whatever she was getting ready to say.

"Then you old enough to know what happened. Fannie Mae was thirteen when she got in trouble the first time. Wasn't her fault either. She got picked up for talking back to a white man. She was buying some things from the grocery store and the storekeeper was trying to cheat her. Now your mama knew her numbers. She wasn't nobody's fool. She knew how to figure, so she called him a liar. He hauled off and slapped her down. Then he had the gall to call the police on her. They took her down to juvenile detention. Chile, it wasn't no fence high enough to keep Fannie Mae where she didn't wanna be. She broke out of that place and hitched a ride to New Orleans. But they caught her and drug her back in a week or two.

"Now your mama's pride was her long pretty hair, a good grade and thick, too. She used to wrap it on top of her head like a crown. When she fixed up you'd swear she was a movie star. When they brought her back the last time, them animals cut all her hair off. Yes m'am, they shaved that poor chile's head clean. Not to be held back, she found a way out again and hooked up with a soldier. They married over in Alabama. That was a joke. Your mama just wanted a way out of that stinking jail. On her honeymoon night she said she made that boy sleep on the porch of his mama's house. She run away from him too. Come back to live with your Aunt Mae. Then trouble seemed to run after her."

Miss Corine kept parting my hair and lathering each gap with Sulphur 8, soothing the tension out of her words. She stopped for a minute to blow her nose and wipe the sweat out of her eyes.

"Baby, I understand why your Big Mama and your aunties ain't told you bout her. The telling hurts. It bring up too many memories. You getting to be a woman now, and God knows you need to hear this. Hold still now. I'm getting ready to put the hot comb to your head."

I held my head down, chin to chest, waiting for the sizzle of hot metal comb on damp, greased naps. Miss Corine's hands were steady, never jerking or burning the tender skin on my neck.

While waiting for Miss Corine to get to the next chapter in Fannie Mae's story, Mr. Pitts from the funeral home next door hollered in the door. "What you know good, Corine?"

"Couldn't be better Pitts. How's business?" Miss Corine hollered back at him.

"Dead as ever," he said, laughing at his own joke.

Big Mama said Mr. Pitts could make a dead man laugh, she said he could make you forget you was mourning somebody. He buried Fannie Mae. I heard folks say he was in love with her. As if she read my mind, when Mr. Pitts left Miss Corine say, "Pitts used to take your mama to the picture show. Buy her all the candy and popcorn she could hold. He really loved your mama like she was his chile. She made him laugh. Where a lot of mens would've taken advantage of a pretty young girl like Fannie Mae, he showed her nothing but kindness and respect, and she give him the same. When she was a lil girl, she was here in my shop messing round or over in the funeral home arranging flowers for Mr. Pitts and Miss Rosa."

There was a quiet space where I spoke my heart.

"I used to hate Fannie Mae," I confessed for the first time to anybody. "I hated her for leaving me and then for being dead. One time I locked myself in the bathroom cause I didn't want to wear no white flower on my new white dress on Mother's Day, letting everybody know my mama was dead. I cried so hard Big Mama felt bad for me. I ended up wearing a red and white flower. Big Mama convinced me how important it was to respect the dead as well as the living."

"I remember that. You almost broke your Big Mama's heart. She knew then how strong you felt bout losing your mama and she felt so helpless, wasn't nothing she could do then."

There was a light tapping on the door and Miss Rosa come in. She was a tiny, elegant lady, like her brother Mr. Pitts. She always wore a hat to match her dress. I wondered if she slept in them hats. Her delicate smile was warm, and her light green eyes invited your confidence and trust. She stepped into the shop gently and looked round for attention like she was bout to make an announcement.

"Corine, on behalf of myself and Mr. Pitts I would like to thank you for the use of your curling irons," Miss Rosa said.

"You been working on Sister Davis, Jessie say."

"Sister Davis was a good Christian woman, a nice-looking woman, but she aged so quickly. All those children I suppose. At any rate, I thank you for your generosity."

"Rosa, you know you welcome to them old irons and anything else I have. When is Sister Davis' funeral?"

"Tomorrow morning, and I do not look forward to dealing with her heathen children. They chose the cheapest casket and arrangements for the dear woman, and I know for a fact that her insurance policy would have more than covered a decent burial." Miss Rosa coughed a delicate cough, then cleared her throat a few times. I took my chance to thank her.

"Miss Rosa, I don't remember my mama very much, but I remember how pretty you made her look for the funeral. Thank you for making her look so nice."

"Why thank you, chile," she said, as if seeing me for the first time. "You look so much like her. She was a lovely girl, so smart and talented. We all loved her. Her passing was a great loss. In all my days I never seen so many grown men cry at a funeral. Mr. Pitts wept the whole time he worked on her. He sent her the money to come home, but she never made it. Didn't she love to dance, Jesus!"

Miss Rosa sniffed and wiped her teary eyes on a black lace hanky she had tied to her wrist.

"She really loved you. She wanted you to be with her. I believe she's much happier with the Lord."

Miss Rosa stood there staring at me for a few minutes, then tossed up her hanky and stepped out the door.

"Everybody loved your mama," Miss Corine went on with her story. "Like I said, she was a good girl, but trouble seemed to follow her."

"What kind of trouble?" I asked, a lil scared of what I might hear.

"When your mama turned fifteen, she got a scholarship to a lil integrated dance school downtown. First of its kind. Run by some crazy white ladies from up North. Fannie Mae and this white girl—Patty, I think her name was—got to be good friends. One day Patty and your mama was holding hands walking in the white folks' park. Fannie Mae forgot all bout them signs and things. She and Patty got to laughing and dancing down the street and over the grass them white folks claimed was theirs. Fannie Mae was so pretty. Too pretty. Some white boys noticed them and asked Patty what she doing holding hands with a nigger. Before they could run or holler or anything, them boys raped them both. Raped them in that lil park down on Main Street in broad daylight. Scarred them girls up for life. Policeman's son."

I was hurting when she said that. My throat tightened up, but I held back the tears. I'd come too far to turn round. "Aunt Mae say all the time, 'Mama's baby, Poppa's maybe,'" I say. "I just want to know bout Fannie Mae."

Miss Corine looked at me in a sad, knowing way and kept on talking.

"There was a big trial, and if the lawyer hadn't a been so scared of that policeman's weight, your mama would've won. She bent after that. But you know she was more determined than ever to keep dancing. She worked out every night after she helped me here in this shop. She was still a chile at fifteen when you was born. Your Big Mama fell in love with you and took to keeping you more than your mama. After a while Fannie Mae felt like she couldn't claim y'all no more. All she had was love, and that don't feed hungry children. She left here and went up North. She found a job cleaning up in a dance hall. Your Big Mama and Aunt Mae felt like it was they fault she died on that dance floor, fell out from a brain tumor, washing away her dreams. Dreams die hard. Some say her spirit broke."

Miss Corine paused with the hot comb in mid-air. I could see her reflection in the mirror, proud chin set tight, eyes trying not to cry. I couldn't hold back no more. I cried till my eyes hurt, till my heart was empty and my soul full. I whispered thanks into the front of Miss Corine's pink uniform, for the pain she had to bear to tell me the truth. She held me close, stroking my hair and rocking me back and forth.

"Now that's all I know, baby. It wasn't all a pretty picture, but it's the one I seen."

Miss Corine wiped my tears and gave me a tissue to blow my nose in. Her rich hands caressed my back and eased the pain that truth could bring.

"If you don't remember nothing else I tell you baby, you remember this: if you got to dance or dream or anything at all, take it a step at a time and don't let nothing and nobody get in your way when you doing right. I ain't saying it's gonna be easy, but we all got a dance to do. You remember this, you hear?"

"Yes m'am," I answered, still wiping away my tears.

Miss Rosa's Monkey

Big Mama said Miss Rosa was the kindest, most soft-spirited soul living on God's green earth, but she had habits that would drive Jesus to take a drink of whiskey. I thought Miss Rosa was a lil different from other folks from being round so many dead people. She and her brother Mr. Pitts ran the funeral home down on Front Street. They learned embalming skills from they father Elijah J. Pitts, also known as Pitts Senior, who founded the business in 1922.

Miss Rosa lived in one of the big, old three-story Victorian houses that ran along Sixth Street between the boardinghouse on the corner and the white house where Miss Tom and Miss Lily lived. The house was the family home of Mr. Pitts and Miss Rosa. They was both born and raised there. Mr. Pitts got married in the green velvet living room. Him and his wife lived with Miss Rosa exactly three months, I was told, before the new Mrs. Pitts said she couldn't live with Miss Rosa's pets. It was her or them. Mr. Pitts and his wife moved the next day into rooms over the funeral home. Mr. Pitts still had supper with his sister once a week, and at noontime every day cept Sunday, Miss Rosa would have a meal with Mr. Pitts and his wife in the rooms over the funeral home while Zack, Mr. Pitts' assistant, sat in one of the cane-bottom rocking chairs on the front porch waiting for somebody to die.

Lots of people thought Miss Rosa was flat-out crazy for having all them animals in her house. It was true that Miss Rosa had a weakness for animals since she was a chile, according to Big Mama, who knowed her back then. She raised chickens, pigeons, parrots, cats, dogs, and even had a lil fish pond in her backyard, next to the pig pen for the Siamese pigs and the black goat that was forever eating the sheets off of Miss Rosa's clothesline and the neighbors' when hers wasn't sweet enough.

The problem for the new Mrs. Pitts was that Miss Rosa's pets sometimes found their way into the most unusual places in the house. Miss Easy, the cat, had a litter in her wedding hat. She woke up one morning with Mr. Louis, the rooster, crowing at the foot of her bed. And when Miss Rosa's pet garter snake, Lady Green, got loose in the house, that was the end of the new Mrs. Pitts' rope. She had to go.

Big Mama say when Miss Rosa was a lil girl she used to get her daddy, Pitts Senior, to lay out her dead pets like people. They sat all round the house, glassy eyes looking over banisters and out from under chairs. Even in the bathroom a family of baby turtles was frozen in time on the back of the commode. Her daddy did it to please her. Then, too, to get her acquainted with methods she was gonna have to use on dead people when she and her brother took over the business. Pretty soon stiff cats, chickens, and fish was all over the house. Miss Rosa's mama had died when she was young so there wasn't nobody to complain, and both her daddy and her brother loved her too much to deny her anything.

Miss Rosa useta dress them animals up like they was dolls. The one time I went to visit her to deliver a pie Big Mama had made, I saw some strange things. Miss Rosa had me wait in the green velvet living room. She called it the library, though there wasn't many books and them that was there looked dusty and old as Miss Rosa. The room was full up with dead animals. Stuffed up. All of em had lil hand-wrote name tags on cardboard. A skinny white rabbit with shiny pink eyes, Miss Texas, was standing on its hind legs wearing a pink fringe skirt and bonnet. There was a brown squirrel, Mr. Busy, in a black cowboy suit; a fat chihuahua, Mr. Sunshine, in a yellow raincoat and four lil yellow rainboots on its paws; and Miss Josephine, a red, green, blue, and yellow parrot wearing a feathered hat and holding a ruffled parasol in its red-painted claw. There was the stiff-necked rooster, Mr. Louis, and a pretty black cat, Mr. Robinson, in a stalking position, one paw stretched out near the tiny face of a stiff white mouse, Mr. White. You had to be there to appreciate the feeling of being in another world, Miss Rosa's special private world.

After she finished high school, Big Mama told me that Miss Rosa learned all parts of the funeral business and started stuffing the dead pets herself. She didn't like to be by herself, so there was always plenty of living cats and canaries, dogs and things running round her yard and all over her house. Pitts Senior died the summer Miss Rosa graduated from college, and even though she was engaged to a doctor from Philadelphia, she come home to take up the business with her brother. She broke off her engagement with the doctor who stayed with Miss Rosa for two days after the funeral. Some folks said he refused to live in the South. Some say he refused to live in the house with all them dead animals.

Her doctor-fiancé left and never come back. Miss Rosa put on a black dress for Pitts Senior's funeral, and that was the only color she wore all the time I knowed her.

I was bout ten years old the spring Miss Rosa got the monkey. Her Cousin Beedle brought it back from Africa where he was a missionary. It was a skinny, hairy brown thing with eyes like a human being and it was always grinning like a rat eating cheese. Miss Rosa was crazy bout that monkey, treat it like it was a chile. It wasn't dead yet, but she dressed it up and had a special silver chain with a red leather collar made for it so she could take it on walks. Big Mama say she had seen some peculiar things in her life but none more funny looking than Miss Rosa walking that hairy brown monkey on a silver chain down Front Street. Some days she'd dress it in a lil straw hat and plaid overalls, sometimes a navy blue sailor outfit. In winter it always wore a heavy black wool coat with gold brass buttons that she ordered special from the Kiddie Shop downtown, where rich white folks shopped for they children. She called him Mr. Please and fed him peanuts and bananas she kept in her patent leather pocketbook. She taught it tricks and said she was teaching him to read. She was put out when Reverend Waters said the monkey couldn't come to church, even if it was dressed up in a suit and tie.

Time passed, and Miss Rosa and Mr. Please continued to live a quiet life between her house, church, and the funeral home. She was near bout sixty-seven when Reverend Gidlaw started courting her. Reverend Gidlaw was a visiting church minister at Eighth Street Baptist Church from Orange, Alabama, thirty miles away. He come to our church once a month to preach that Sunday's sermon. He was a skinny brown man, who looked kinda like a monkey hisself, and he had a thick moustache that he useta twirl round between his thin paw-looking fingers. The lil black-frame glasses he wore always seemed like they was bout to fall off the end of his nose. After the Sundays he preached, he used to walk Miss Rosa round the corner to her front gate. Mr. Please walked between them. When Reverend Gidlaw tried to help her up a curb or be so bold as to try to hold her hand, Mr. Please would try to bite him and start screeching at him in monkey talk.

One Sunday Miss Rosa invited Reverend Gidlaw to supper. He brought flowers for her and a huge bunch of ripe yellow bananas for Mr. Please. They had a big supper on fried chicken, green peas, mashed potatoes, collard greens, cornbread, sweet potato pie for dessert, and a taste of blackberry wine to wash it all down. To the Reverend's surprise, Mr. Please sat at the table with them, using a knife and fork on his fried chicken.

Everything went alright till Mr. Please sneaked some of that blackberry wine and start swinging from the chandelier. Miss Rosa tried to ignore him, then she tried to persuade him with sweet words and treats to come down, but Mr. Please was full of food and a whole lot more. Mr. Please was enjoying hisself. His last move was to leap from the ceiling and land on Reverend Gidlaw's back just as a forkful of greens was going in the Reverend's mouth. Before he could put his fork down, Mr. Please had peed a big smelly spot on the back of the Reverend's suit and was jumping up and down spraying his hat. Miss Rosa was the most embarrassed she had ever been in her life. She was mad, too. She put Mr. Please in the bedroom and tried to drown out his monkey screams with gospel singing on the radio. Reverend Gidlaw soon left, almost running with his hat in his hand.

After this incident, Big Mama asked Miss Rosa what most probably was wrong with Mr. Please. Sick? Crazy? Too many greens?

"None of that. Mr. Please was just another jealous bastard. That monkey almost cost me to mess up my last chance at a lil romance. I'm old but I ain't dead yet."

Reverend Gidlaw went home to pray. Miss Rosa prayed too before she put Mr. Please to sleep. She dressed him up in a black suit just like Reverend Gidlaw's, and glasses like his too. As a matter fact, when Miss Rosa was done Mr. Please was the spitting image of the Reverend.

"Who say you can't have your cake and eat it too? Ain't that right Reverend?" Miss Rosa said to the monkey, the first, last, and only time I was ever in her house.

Spit In The Governor's Tea

December 1959 was the year Miss Shine got even for 400-year-old wrongs. I was born that year, so the story was told to me and long as I'm Black I'll never forget it. Every Christmas Eve when Big Mama and all the other grown folks went shopping downtown, Justine Baker would come to our apartment to sit with me. Even though she was only in her twenties, she could tell stories good as Aunt Mae, Big Mama, and Aunt Vi. I especially liked the one she told me every Christmas Eve, the one bout Miss Shine.

Justine was a lil on the plump side cause she had a terrible sweet tooth. She wore loose cotton housedresses, with pockets that hid penny candy, and big pink curlers in her hair every day but Sunday when she sang in the choir. Her voice was soprano and real pretty so she usually had the star position in the choir stand as the soloist. I loved hearing her catch notes with her voice and then letting them fly over our heads in the congregation, like birds. When Justine was telling a story her voice was like that too—high, sweet, and strong.

After I got in my red footie pajamas, brushed my teeth, and said my prayers, Justine would light Big Mama's kerosene lamp, put me in the middle of Big Mama's bed, and sit looking at me from Big Mama's rocking chair. She would fold her plump hands in her lap and rock slow, backward and forward as she told me Miss Shine's story.

"'Round Christmastime there's a whole lotta things in the air you cain't see. Things that make you smile at folks you don't even know and speak to your worst enemy. People get in what you call the Christmas Spirit. I'd like to think it was the Christian spirit and folks would do it every day of the year, but the world just ain't like that. This Christmas spirit infect everybody like a disease. Everything is amazement.

"Well, this particular December I'm gonna tell you bout wasn't much different. At the start of December our chorus teacher told my class we had been chose to sing Christmas carols at the governor's mansion. For weeks all the kids that lived in the projects talked bout was the school chorus singing at the governor's mansion on Christmas Eve. Glo Dean, Jimmy, Pearl, and me was all in the choir at church, too, so everybody knowed we would make our mamas proud.

"Your Big Mama was just as excited as everybody else, but when she heard she couldn't help but say out loud, 'With all the mess the governor been stirring up, standing in the schoolhouse door to keep our children from a equal education. Now the children gonna have opportunity to show him they know a lil something already.'

"'Amen,' Miss Shine broke in. 'I'm gonna be there to see our children show out. The governor done asked me already to stay past sundown on Christmas Eve.'

"Miss Shine had worked in the governor's mansion ever since her husband, Mr. Polk, died and left her with no insurance money and a heap of bills to pay. When Mr. Polk was living, he useta cuss a mean blue streak when Miss Shine spoke bout working.

"'What you wanna work for?' he would scream, so everybody in the neighborhood could hear and know he was a man.

"'What you mean? I work every day. I near bout break my back cleaning up after you. We got bills to pay, and I want some nice things round here. Like some new curtains on the window, stead of that old sheet I sewed up so folks couldn't look in, a flower garden, and a new hat for church once in a while.'

"'Shine, where can you work? On your rusty knees in some white folks' kitchen? Bringing they nasty clothes in my house? No m'am. I ain't gonna stand for you working for white folks as long as I can swing this hammer,' he would end up, swinging his railroad hammer over his bald head.

"Mr. Polk worked on the railroad for over thirty years. When he died and couldn't swing his hammer no more, Miss Shine had to work. All she knowed was keeping house and cooking, so when Miss Emma Lou told her bout the job at the governor's mansion she ain't hesitated but a minute. Miss Shine was kinda nervous bout working in a place as fancy as the governor's mansion, but Miss Emma Lou straightened her out quick.

" 'Honey chile, the governor and his wife is simple country crackers. They don't put on airs till foreigners come round. They eat, sleep, and pee out a hole just like anybody else. You member that and you'll do alright,' Miss Emma Lou said.

" 'But all them fancy place settings, three or four different kinda forks and spoons, pouring tea before supper . . . I just don't know, Emma Lou.'

" 'Colored folks, as you know, is the most amazing people on this earth. Anything we put our minds to and our hearts into, we can get done good and most times better than that. You'll never if you can do a thing till you try, and a try has never failed.'

"Miss Emma Lou finished her speech by spitting in her spit cup like she always do.

" 'Emma Lou, I'll do the best I kin. Thank you for the blessing.'

"Miss Shine got the job, and she caught on quick. The funniest thing she had to do was pouring tea. Every day round four o'clock the governor's wife Emmie rung a silver bell. That was Miss Shine's signal to pour boiling water in a great big silver teapot that sit on a big silver tray set with easy-to-break china cups and saucers and real silver spoons.

"Every day the governor say the same thing. 'Shine, pour me up a cupful, with round bout six spoons of sugar. I like mine sweet as Miss Emmie here.'

"If there wasn't no company, Miss Emmie would crow like a rooster and say, 'Doggone if it ain't tea time again. Cheers, daddy.'

"They would sit in the living room, quiet as two rocks in a river cept for the slurping of that sweet tea, for exactly thirteen minutes. Then Miss Emmie would ring her lil silver bell, and Miss Shine would either pour some more tea or roll the cart back in the kitchen. Madam Waters, the head cook, would start heaping food in serving dishes, and Miss Shine would take off her white apron and start walking to the bus stop. It was a mile and a half easy. She'd wait with the other maids who worked after four o'clock for the last bus to town. From downtown she'd have to catch another bus home to the projects.

"Weeks before the first Christmas pine was chopped for decoration, Miss Shine was in charge of polishing cabinets full of silver, starching closets full of linen, and her biggest job—but the one she loved the best and saved for last—was cleaning the grand French crystal chandelier that hung in the main entry hall to the mansion. She said cleaning the 814 crystals all by hand give her time to think. Her chandelier cleaning ritual went something like this:

"'I climb the ladder with my cleaning bucket in one hand. Once I git to the top I untwists the wire that thread through a lil bitty hole in the crystal head. The wire hold the crystal on the big brass tiered circles. I put many crystals as I kin in the bucket. Then I soaks em in ammonia and lemon juice. Then I rinses em with real hot water and lay em on clean white towels. Then I polish em with spit and a soft flannel cloth till they shine like pure diamonds.'

"Two days before the singing, a strong feeling pass over Miss Shine like something bad was bout to happen. She was sitting on top of the ladder in the entry hall taking the crystals down. She said it was like a heavy cloud press down on her and hung on her heart. She was near bout done up there so she eased down off the ladder and set up in the kitchen pantry polishing them chandelier crystals with spit and shining em with a white flannel rag. She polished the big round crystal with a thousand faces that was big as a Florida grapefruit with special care, rubbing it like she used to rub on Mr. Polk's bald head to get him to go to sleep at night. It hung from the middle of the chandelier. She spit-shined and rag-rubbed till she could see her face, that was the color of a grocery sack, in every flat edge like a mirror.

"Christmas Eve day the snow started falling round noon. Fat, white flakes covered the ground like one of Aunt Judy's wedding quilts. The governor and his family invited some friends and neighbors over to the mansion to have a early supper. Just as they was finishing they meal, the three yellow school buses rolled round the circle driveway and parked on the side in the bus parking spaces. The governor, Miss Emmie, and they few friends went out on the front porch to watch the first group assemble round that twenty-five-foot Christmas tree all decorated and lit up in the middle of that lawn all covered with snow. Miss Shine dried her hands on her apron and stood in the front window looking out from behind the curtains, her heart near bout busting with joy. She knowed we was gonna do her proud that night.

"The first group of them white children sang they Christmas carols in high-pitched cut-off notes that didn't sound right to us, nor Miss Shine, but she clapped when they was done with 'Jingle Bells,' 'We Wish You a Merry Christmas,' and 'White Christmas,' even though they messed up them songs like broke glass on bicycle tires.

"The second group wasn't much better. They was from a church-run school, so they sang a lot of hymns. Like the first group, every one of em was white and dressed just alike in blue jackets, with pants for the boys and skirts for the girls. Miss Shine wasn't impressed, but she clapped for them, too.

"Then us colored children broke loose. We arranged ourselves round that Christmas tree, holding hands in a circle. We was wearing long white robes with gold sashes over our shoulders looking like black angels. Miss Shine felt faint. 'Oh Come All Ye Faithful,' 'Away in a Manger,' 'Oh Holy Night,' and just when she thought she couldn't take no more heavenly sounds, I led the choir in 'Silent Night.' When I was done there was a deep hush, quiet like even God had stopped what She was doing to listen. I was feeling the spirit cause God was leading that song. Miss Shine almost forgot where she was. She clapped long and loud, put her hand over her heart, and kept clapping on her hip with her free hand even when we was heading for our bus. She could see Glo Dean, Jimmy, Pearl, me, and the others dancing round that tree like we was at home round the chinaberry tree in July.

"The governor went out on the lawn as we was gathering near

our separate buses. I remember it clear as day. The governor's speech went something like this:

" 'That was some real nice caroling children. You all did a fine job. How bout another round of applause for everybody.'

"He said *everybody* like it hurt him, then he said, 'I would like to take this opportunity to invite Middle T. Morris School and St. Joseph's Academy to join my wife and myself and our guests in the mansion for a cup of hot chocolate. That was some mighty fine singing from my alma mater and rival school. Come on in children. Merry Christmas to you.'

"He waved the white children over to the front door and welcomed them with a handshake into the entry hall of the mansion.

"Something inside of Miss Shine broke in two when she saw our faces. Glo Dean and the others looked soft and sad like they was gonna cry. Jimmy's face was hard, like he wanted to pitch a brick through the front windows of the mansion. Pearl looked like she didn't spect no less. I was just too shame to look anywhere but down at the ground. I couldn't believe that after he heard God in my song he could be so mean and cold-hearted.

"Miss Emmie rushed into the entry hall and found Miss Shine still as a stature standing at the window staring at the white children lining up at the door and the colored bus pulling outta sight down the driveway.

" 'Shine, quick, fix the children some hot chocolate. There seems to be bout thirty-five of em. Not too much sugar now, or the lambs will be up all night,' Miss Emmie said, sweet as Brer Fox in the briar patch.

"Miss Shine walked to the kitchen with lead feet, like a woman without her mind. She fixed the hot chocolate rattling pots and pans, dropping the silver, and spilling milk all over the floor. She was madder than a foam-mouth dog, but what could she do? She poured the hot chocolate into thirty-five white dixie cups for thirty-five thin pink lips to drink from. Her hands was trembling and her head felt light. Her blood pressure was rising. She kept thinking that they was all just children. Why couldn't the governor see that? Color don't matter in the sight of God. The governor think he know more than God?

"When all the cups was full and on the rolling tea cart, Miss

Shine, pushed it slow into the entry hall. She heard one of the white kids say something bout *sending the niggers back to the jungle* and heard laughing break out round the room and saw wide grins on the governor and Miss Emmie's faces. Each one of em took a cup without even a thank you or a look in Miss Shine's direction. She left it in the Lord's hands, and She come through. With no warning, the big round crystal that hung from the middle of the chandelier fell with a loud crack on the marble floor, breaking into a million pieces. Miss Shine's mouth dropped open and her eyes got big. It didn't hurt nobody, but she took it to be a sign.

" 'Them niggers must've sent a voodoo in here on us,' one of the girls said, giggling nervouslike. Miss Shine fixed a look on that chile that made her turn red as a beet and start to cry.

"Miss Emmie seen Miss Shine staring at that chile and snapped up, 'Shine get a broom and sweep up this mess before one of these children gets hurt.'

"She was trying to break Miss Shine's spell on the child, and she did, but Miss Shine turned to stare Miss Emmie full in the face for a long uncomfortable minute before going back in the kitchen.

"Miss Shine come back and parted the crowd with the point of her broom, waving it wild, just missing knocking a few blond heads and poking out a few blue eyes. She swept up every sliver of crystal she could find. Then she put the pieces in a paper sack. After collecting all the empty cups and cleaning up the kitchen, she walked that mile and a half through the snow to a main street. She hailed a taxi that took her home. The streets was mostly empty, as it was near nine o'clock. It was cold and snow was still falling.

"When she got in her apartment she turned the oven on and opened the door to warm up the kitchen. Then she pulled out a chair and stood on it. She felt round up on the top kitchen shelf for a fat white candle she had bought at a spiritual store years before for the purpose of a ritual Miss Mary told her to do, but she never did. She sat down with it at the kitchen table, still in her coat dripping with snow. She lit the candle and sit there staring at it. She poured the broke up crystal from the paper sack onto a piece of newspaper spread out on the table and looked at em while talking to herself. Them pieces of crystal still sparkled like diamonds, but every jagged edge was like a dagger in her heart. Miss Shine sit at her kitchen table till Christmas morning broke light, sit there till the thing she had to do come to her.

" 'Folks say things changed, but it's still like slavery times.' Miss Shine's mind eased way, way back. She heard a chant far off, deep as slave graves and old as Africa.

"*Blood boiled thick, run red like a river, slaves scream, wail, moan after their dead. Daddy lynched, mama raped, baby sister sold down river. Slaves scream, wail, moan after their dead. The cook know what to do to save the race, stop the screams, save the blood from boiling thick, running red like a river.*

"Miss Shine all of a sudden knowed what she had to do to save the race. It come to her like in a dream, but it was real. It was a story told to her a long time ago. In slavery times the cook had a heap of power. They stole food to feed the children to keep em from dying before they was sold off. Fed the mens scraps of lean meat to give em the strength to find freedom and bring it back home. The cook had the power to poison the master, too. When the beatings, killings, and selling off of families was too much to bear, often time the cook would use her knowledge of herbs and roots to make her white master sick, sometimes die.

"Miss Shine was possessed by her power. She snatched off her coat and white apron and went into her bedroom to get the wood bowl her mama give her and the iron head of Mr. Polk's hammer. She came back to the table spread with all that broke crystal and ground it up with the head of the hammer in her mama's wood bowl. She ground it till sweat dripped off her face into the bowl. She ground it till the crystals was fine as dust and tied the pile of it in a corner of her slip. She burnt the bowl in her tin bathtub and flushed the ashes down the toilet. Then she wrapped the hammerhead in flannel and put it away.

"*Nobody know how the master get sick. Nobody know how he die. The doctors won't know why he pain so in his stomach. The grind be so fine. He think it be root work and be scared of niggers from then on.* The cooks kept whispering in her ears, chanting.

"When Miss Shine had to go back to work after New Year's, she was ready, almost happy. All the other women on the maids' bus was grumbling bout having to go back to work.

" 'Somebody got to pay them bill collectors,' a voice in the back of the bus hollered out. That put everybody in a good mood. Miss Shine was really wanting to get to the mansion that morning.

"Miss Emmie stopped her from washing the lunch dishes to tell her they was having a guest to dinner and he was gonna have tea with em. Miss Shine *yes m'amed* her, looking direct in her eyes. Miss Emmie wasn't used to coloreds making eye contact, and she near bout run out the kitchen. Miss Shine went on as usual fixing tea. She put the kettle on to boil.

"*Blood boil thick . . .*

"She kept hearing the whispers. She poured the boiling water over the tea leaves and strained it into the big silver teapot.

"*Run red like a raging river . . .*

"She took down three china cups with a flower pattern and set em straight on matching saucers.

"*Nobody know how the master get sick . . .*

"Miss Shine put everything on the big tea cart.

"*Nobody know how he die . . .*

"She untied the knot in the corner of her slip, emptied the powder into the sugar bowl, and stirred it up good.

"*You done good sister . . . you done right . . . we can rest now. . . .* That was the last whisper.

"Miss Shine smile before she serve the governor, Miss Emmie, and they stone-face guest, a south Georgia mayor with a beer belly and a mouth full of *nigras.* Miss Shine kept pouring tea for the governor and Miss Emmie for more than two weeks before she disappeared.

"Some folks say she move to a entirely colored town in Texas. Other folks say she wasn't really of this world in the first place. Nobody living ever see Miss Shine again. She told me this story the day Aunt Judy sent me to her house with a piece of Christmas cake, two days before she disappeared.

"The doctor that examined the governor couldn't find nothing wrong with him. As delicate as she look, Miss Emmie musta had a iron stomach, she wasn't but a lil bit sick. The governor suffered stomach pains for the rest of his life. He got cancer of the intestines at the age of seventy-two and died after a long and painful sickness.

"From then on, the school chorus started singing Christmas carols at the colored nursing home every year to honor our own folk. Nobody never talk bout wanting to sing for the governor no more. Every time I sing 'The Spirit Can Move' solo, I dedicate it to Miss Shine, wherever she is. Always remember your ancestors."

The Blues Ain't Nothin
But A Good Woman Feelin Bad

A lady named Miss Blue lived down the block from us. She useta sit on her front porch watching TV from eight o'clock in the morning till near dark. First thing in the morning she come out her door in a short housedress in summer, or a raggedy-edged wool robe in winter, with pink sponge hair rollers in her short graying hair and a Kool cigarette hanging from between her lips. In wintertime she'd be carrying a coffee cup with Irish whiskey in it; in the summer a can of beer in a brown paper sack. She would set her cup or can on the porch next to her newspaper, then haul out her lil black-and-white TV and put it on top of the big gray metal garbage can two feet in front of her. Miss Blue didn't want to miss nothing. Not "Edge of Night" or "Days of Our Lives" or Miss Alice putting Mr. Henry outdoors again.

Miss Blue had real dark skin, blue-black Aunt Mae say. Her eyes was muddy brown, and the whites was really yellow with red veins in them. She was older than Big Mama, but you'd have to look hard for a wrinkle on her—her skin was tight as new leather. Her face was puffed up from years of drinking and sad from being lonesome.

Sometimes I'd sit on the porch with her in the summertime to watch a few of the soap opera stories on her TV. Her favorite was "Edge of Night." She knew them people better than she knew herself. They were like family to her, since her only son had died years before and her daughter, she say, had slipped through a crack in the world and she ain't heard from her since she run off from home at fifteen with a piano man. Miss Blue would talk to the characters on TV like they was listening. She would shake her finger at them like they was standing on the porch next to her.

"Erica, you know you ain't got no business breaking up that man and his wife. It don't make no sense for you to be so mean." She would fuss. Sometimes she would jump straight up off of her chair and scream at one of the characters to look out for a murderer behind them, or yell to the jury that they sending the wrong woman to prison, or give advice to the confused. After being round her awhile, I got used to her. When the stories went off at four o'clock, she'd turn the sound down on the TV and talk to me. No talking was allowed cept at the folks on TV during the story hours, and only talk bout the story during commercial breaks.

At night I'd hear her singing the blues sitting on her front porch or at her back window and I would sleep easy with her rough, low voice wrapped round me in my dreams. Miss Blue used to sing the blues for a living till her heart started failing. She'd lived through three heart attacks. She might've told me this story cause Jill, on one of the stories, was left at the altar embarrassed cause Peter, who was supposed to marry her, called her at the church from a phone booth to say he'd changed his mind, or it might've been cause it was June when it happened to her, but something set Miss Blue off on the past and she started talking bout love and pain. The way she talked, there wasn't one without the other.

"I been in love too many times to count. If love was a dollar bill I'd be a millionaire, and if pain was a quarter it'd be triple. All I got now is my memories—some good, some bad. You know I know how Jill feel, like her throat been cut. I know cause it happen to me almost like that in June of 1923."

Miss Blue lit another cigarette and took a swig of beer before she went on. She looked in the palm of her hand and traced what she told me was her love line. I could see that it was broken and not very long.

"Me and Bo Willie Peeks met in a juke joint I was singing in, down by Kin Folks Corner. I wasn't no more than twenty-four or twenty-five years old, and he was the first man I really let love me and the first man I truly give my heart and soul to. Now there was plenty mens round panting like puppy dogs, lapping at my heels waiting for a sign of crumbs. Mens that made me feel like a star. But Bo Willie took my mind. I knowed he was whorish. When I met him, he was married and tipping out on his wife. I never figured he'd tip out on me, and that was my downfall.

"He come to the Dew Drop Inn where I was singing and he would sit at a table up front making love to me with his eyes. Chills run up and down my spine when I catch his eyes all over me like that. Wasn't long before he was waiting for me after the show. I was still living at home with my mama and wasn't nobody round me then. One night he come up to me at the bar and he says, 'Hey sweetmeat, what's cooking?' I didn't know what he was talking bout. I wasn't hip then. So I mumbles, 'Ain't nothing cooking yet.' I was so nervous, sweat start popping off my face, turning my hair back. 'You what's cooking, sugar pie. Your cooking is fine as wine and you look good enough to eat, mama.' That man drowned me with sweet words and kindness. Treat me like a queen and set me up on a throne. I wasn't useta that kinda treatment. You see I knowed I was jet black and didn't have no hips and wasn't particularly pretty and my breasts wasn't big as sugar tits, but he made me feel like I was the most beautiful Black creature breathing air, and I almost believed him. He was the one made me feel like I was somebody special. Bo Willie was a man's man. Don't get me wrong, he wasn't nowhere near perfect. He drank a lil, smoke that old weed too. That make him crazy sometimes, and he'd be mean to me, call me a ugly baboon, or talk bout my bug eyes and flat feet, or my mama if he was in a real bad way. But usually he was good to me. Give me money, buy me whiskey. He begged me on his hands and knees, çlinging to my skirt tail, to marry him. I didn't really feel ready, but he kept on bout how good we was together, how much he love me, and how much he could do for me. After awhile love did cloud my eyes up.

"Bo Willie got a good-paying job on the railroad as a porter and said he was through swinging. He was ready to settle down, with me. When he'd come home from the railroad he'd take me out to dinner at Fat Daddy's, or over to your Aunt Mae's for a drink, then we'd go dancing and git a cheap hotel room and make love for days on end till he had to hit the road again. He'd bring me dresses from New York and Philly, send me train tickets to meet him when he was lonesome.

"Finally I give in and told him I'd marry him. We almost broke that hotel bed celebrating the engagement. Our lovemaking was like two freight trains meeting head on. Chile, he was my thunder and honey. He was all I could see, smell, taste, or touch. I couldn't think bout him without getting a good strong feeling warming in my belly. We made plans to get married the day he got back from a three-week trip up to New York. I told my mama, all the boys in the band, and the bar owner so he'd let me off on a weekend for my honeymoon. I was so happy I smiled all the time, and strangers on the street started asking me if I was in love. I couldn't do nothing but shake my head and grin.

"He called me that first week saying he was lonesome. 'I'm lonesome too,' I say to him. 'I only got eyes for you Bo Willie.'

" 'These gals in New York bout to drive me crazy. A man cain't go to a bar for a drink without em all over me,' he say, teasing.

" 'I hope you tell em you good as married,' I tease him back.

" 'I do, but it don't matter none to these gals in New York,' he say, laughing.

"I wasn't worried. He was a good man. Told me he was tired of running round and wanted a wife and a settled life, and I was ready to kiss his feets and bear him a house full of children till my body was weak. They would've been love children for sure.

"A week before he was due back I went shopping for my wedding dress—a real expensive white wool suit with pearl buttons—and white gloves, shoes, pocketbook, and hat to match. I had to admit I looked good, sharp as a tack. I even bought a lil see-through nightgown for the wedding night and got some love oil from Miss Mary to keep his nature up all night.

"The day Bo Willie was to arrive at my mama's house for the wedding, one hour before the preacher and guests was to come, Bo Willie call me and told me he had another gal. It was like a ax to my head. His words cut me to the bone. He say he still love me, but he met this woman who must've put a root on him cause he couldn't explain why he done what he did. He say he didn't want me to marry him and be miserable. Hmph! I loved that man so much I told him I didn't care bout no other woman, I'd take him like he was if only he'd come to the house that minute and say yes before the preacher. He said he was still in New York and didn't know if he was really ready to settle down. I ask him if I could come where he was so we could talk, and he flat-out refused. Then I got mad, remembering his sweet lies of loving me to the grave.

" 'Bo Willie, you a no-good lying dog. You a bastard like your daddy and if you was on fire, I wouldn't waste my spit on you. You evil muther-fucker. I hope you die choking on your own vomit. You have made a hard bed, now lay in it. You gonna be sorry though, you gonna miss me. Everything you touch is gonna turn to shit, dry up like dust and blow on the wind.'

"I could hear him crying on the other end saying 'God no!' He believed in roots and knowed I was putting a cussing on him that clorox wasn't gonna bleach off. I slammed the phone down and cried for two days solid. For a week I didn't sleep, eat more than a slice of dry bread and a half cup of coffee. Food lumped up in my throat thinking bout him with another woman. It almost drove me mad. I'd wake up in the middle of the night calling his name, talked to myself out loud. I walked the streets in all kinds of weather looking for him. I knew he'd come back, maybe with that bitch that stole him. I really didn't hate her so much. It was him that hurt me, and wasn't no telling what he'd done told her. I wanted him dead though, boiling in his own blood. I wanted him to hurt my hurt.

"One night I was walking the streets, going from joint to joint trying to find him, and I saw him. He was by hisself, getting outta a brand new fishtail Cadillac outside of Fat Daddy's. I rushed over to the car and swung open the door on his side. I know I scared him cause I looked like a haint. My hair was standing up on my head, I hadn't changed my clothes for three days, and my eyes had murder in em. I snatched him out the car and was quick on him like white on rice. I hadn't had no food in days but I found the strength to knock him to the ground. Then I got in the car, shifted in reverse, and tried to run him down like the dog he was. He was lucky I smashed into a telephone pole fore I flattened his ass. I just broke his leg and run over his foot.

"I wasn't hurt, so I got out the car and walked home with my head up. Took a long hot bath when I got there and lit a seven-day candle to ask to be released from him and get my mind back. I come back to myself, but I left part of me back at that wreck. I'd had my part of love. After that blow all I needed was somebody to keep the cold off me at night. Love hurt. I really had something to sing the blues bout then. That same year I made a hit record, my only record, 'The Blues Ain't Nothin but a Good Woman Feelin Bad.' . . . "

Miss Blue stood up, put one hand on her good hip, and pointed her finger at the TV. "Yes chile, I know how Jill feel standing on that altar by herself, just like a stone has lodged in her chest, beating against her broke heart."

The street lights were starting to come on. Miss Blue put out her cigarette and tossed the empty beer can in the trash can under the TV. She looked down at me and added one last thought before turning in for the evening.

"I heard a few months after I wrecked his car and run over his foot that the woman he was with took all his money and left him and he lost his job on the railroad." Miss Blue paused. You know something baby, I hope to this day that sorry son-of-a-bitch is still sucking rocks. One good thing done come out of all that though, and that was a song. It was blue but it was a song. A damn good one, too."

Then she started to singing real low, the song that come out of passing through the blues over love.

Funny Women

Miss Tom was not a pretty woman, she was handsome like a man. Tall, broad-shouldered, big-boned, lean and lanky like a man. Her soft silver hair was cut short and curled tight round her narrow face that was smooth and honey brown. She had silver sideburns, thick eyebrows that almost met across the top of her face, dark black eyes that could see through almost anything, and a silver mustache, like a man. Kids, and some grownfolks, who didn't know Miss Tom was always asking her if she be man or woman. Miss Tom was patient with small children and strangers, so she would say in a deep, husky voice, "Don't judge a book by looking at the cover." Her chest was flat as a man's, her hands was big, thick, and calloused. But she had a woman's eyes, dark black eyes that held woman secrets, eyes that had seen miracles and reflected love like only a woman can. Her walk was slow and deliberate—like she had somewhere to go but wasn't in no hurry to get there.

Me and Miss Tom was friends, good friends. She taught me how to fish, throw a knife, tie knots, tame birds, and believe in a world of impossibilities. She lived in a big white house next door to Miss Rosa. It was a nice old house with long porches that wrapped round the sides, with green shutters behind where lace curtains whipped in the breeze. She had lived there with Miss Lily for as long as I can remember.

Miss Lily was real sick, in the hospital with a fever. Big Mama say doctors don't know nothing, so it wasn't no surprise that they say Miss Tom couldn't even visit her cause what she had *might* be catching. They didn't know what she had.

When Miss Tom come by our house with a fishing rod over her shoulder headed for the river, I asked her if I could go. She nodded her head and waited under the chinaberry tree in the yard while I went in to ask Big Mama and get my fishing pole.

As I come out, Big Mama stuck her head out the door and hollered at Miss Tom. "Hey Tom, how you making out? I hear Miss Lily sick. You need anything?"

"I'm doing pretty good so far. Me and your young'un going to catch my supper, and yours too, I reckon." Miss Tom winked down at me.

"You tell Lily we all praying for her when you get chance to see her."

"Thank you. I preciate your prayers and I'll tell her you praying for her. We all is. See you fore sundown."

"Tom, don't you drop my baby over in the river. She got some things to do round this house when she gets back. Y'all take care." Big Mama waved us on.

I put my hand in Miss Tom's, and she held it kind of light like she might break it.

"I'm sorry bout Miss Lily," I say, and squeeze her hand.

"Me too, baby. You and me both," she say, squeezing back.

It was early in May and spring was in every strawberry bush, chinaberry tree, and lime-colored leaf. The sky was crispy deep blue and full of white fluffy clouds. The sun was so bright it hurt my eyes to look at anything white or shiny. Down by the river was quiet, nobody round but us.

"What we got to catch with today?" I asked Miss Tom.

"We got a sardine, some vienna sausages, and fresh bacon," she said, laughing that deep rough laugh of hers. "These old crafty swimmers do like that fresh bacon." Then, like she remembered something terrible, the smile and the light in her face dried up.

I guessed Miss Tom was worried bout Miss Lily. Her mind seemed to be miles off. I thought she and Miss Lily was kin or sisters for the longest. It was the only reasoning I could make out, them living together like that. When I asked Aunt Mae if they was sisters, she say, "They sisters alright, but it ain't by blood." I didn't know what she meant so I left it alone then. I knew Miss Tom was different from other women and not just cause of her moustache and the mannish way she walk or the deep husky way she talk. She was just different. I heard folks say she and Miss Lily was funny, but I never noticed nothing funny bout either one of them. They was serious women.

In silence Miss Tom fed our hooks and we threw the lines in. We leaned back into the shade of a pine tree on a soft bed of pine needles. Afterwhile the sun caught us strong in the face. Miss Tom squinted directly into the sun, and when I looked up a few minutes later, tears were running down her face like twin rivers.

"Miss Tom, you alright?" I asked, taking her big rough hand in mine, trying to give her some comfort.

She heaved a few times, like she was gonna let out a shout, then she got up and walked to the edge of the river bank and stood there looking in. Her back was to me. She breathed deep with her whole body a few times, then calmed down easy and come back to sit next to me. She wiped her face with a clean white handkerchief. After, she blew her nose in it.

"I got a lot on my mind baby, but Miss Tom ain't gonna jump in yet. I needs to clear my head. Miss Juliette heavy on my mind."

"Who Miss Juliette?" I asked. "You mean Miss Lily."

"Miss Juliette is the most beautiful creature on God's green earth. She better get over this fever, we got things to do, we got plans. We going back to New Orleans . . .," Miss Tom said, like I wasn't there.

She was quiet for a few minutes, but I kept my eye on her cause I was real confused. I never heard tell of nobody round named Miss Juliette. Now, Miss Tom don't talk much. Say she don't like to waste words saying nothing. But without warning, out of nowhere, without me even asking, she dived deep into a story, just like I wasn't there, simply cause there was a story that needed telling. She began in that husky, deep voice of hers that would've put me to sleep, cept the story kept me on the edge of them pine needles and my eyes steady on Miss Tom.

"I growed up in a house with six brothers on the banks of the Mississippi River. Six mens and me till Mama had Juliette. I member it like it was yesterday . . . the midwife coming in the middle of the night, sending the boys out, and making me boil water and tear up sheets. Way afterwhile I heard Mama in the bedroom hollering, then grunting like her bowels wanna move, then I hear a baby crying. I peep behind the curtain in time to see the midwife holding up a ugly lil wrinkled-up red baby. It was clear to be a white man's chile, most probably Mr. Boone who Mama kept house for.

Mama called her Juliette after Mr. Boone's dead wife. It was a pretty name for such a ugly lil worm as that. My name rough, fit me like a glove—Tom. My grandmama's mama name me after her mama, Tomasina Louise Perry. That's what was wrote in the family Bible. But since I was lil, the boys and Mama call me Tom and treat me like I was a boy, no different from the other six. I believe sometimes even my ma forgot.

"I was five years old when Juliette was born, but I was the one learnt to bathe her, feed her, and sit up all night with her by the fire, rocking with her till she could sleep. She growed into such a pretty chile. Long black hair Mama kept in two plaits, so soft I would rub my face in it, taking deep breaths of it, trying to take her in. She was a white man's chile alright, her skin was white as Jesus Christ's. She was built slim, but strong and long-legged, and them eyes of hers was green and gold like cats' eyes. You look in em too deep and you was liable to get sucked in. She was strong-willed, and we spoiled her rotten by giving her everything she thought she wanted.

"Yes m'am, she growed to be pretty as a picture. I was proud to walk the two miles into town with her on my back to show her off. Folks who didn't know us ask me who chile she was. When I say she my sister, they fall out laughing. When she say this my sister Tom, they laugh more, cause I looked like a boy even then.

Even then I woulda cut my arm to the sleeve to please her. When she was four she demanded we call her Miss Juliette. The poor chile thought she really was white. To keep our precious Juliette happy we called her Miss Juliette, Queen of the Mississippi, till she wasn't round to call no more.

"After Juliette was born, Mama had to go work in Mr. Boone's fields picking cotton. That left mostly me to take care of Miss Juliette. We slept in the same bed every night for sixteen years. For sixteen years we never spent a night apart. I never loved nobody like Miss Juliette, nobody. . . . "

Miss Tom stopped. She kept looking up at the sun and staring out at the water like she was blind. Finally, she pulled a corncob pipe from the front pocket of her overalls and a pouch of sweet-smelling tobacco outta her back pocket. Without even looking down to see what her hand was doing, she pinched a bit of tobacco and stuffed it into the bowl of the pipe that was cradled in her other hand. She struck a match on the bottom of her boot, and for a few minutes we was swallowed in a cloud of sweet smoke. then a strange thing happened. Miss Tom said some things to make me know she was way off somewhere, cause the next thing outta her mouth opened up a world of what I thought was impossibles and never-even-dreamed-ofs.

"I don't member how we started loving one another different. Who made the first move. It just seemed like we was always in love and loving one another. Sometimes I'd think bout her being my blood sister and worry bout going to hell for loving her in such a sinful way. I think it happened . . . yeah . . . it was the summer it was too hot to sleep. The summer the boys was all out possum hunting with Uncle Trey, and Mama was sleeping by Mr. Boone's house. I musta been thirteen and Juliette was bout eight. It was so dog-awful hot and nobody was home cept us so we figured it was safe to sleep naked. My sweet lil sister turned to me, and in her sweet lil whispering voice she say, 'Tom hold me to you like you do when its cold.'

" 'It's too hot to be all hugged up, Miss Juliette. Go on to sleep,' I said to her kinda rough. Then I was sorry cause her feelings was hurt and she start to whining like a broke record and I couldn't refuse her nothing. It was all in a natural move that I cradled up next to her lil body spoon fashion. Somehow in the middle of the night, we was laying face to face, me still holding her in my arms. By the moonlight she was almost too pretty to look at and so creamy white like a angel. I member I closed my eyes and counted stars. Afterwhile I felt a soft something all over me, tingly kinda. I could feel the berries stand up on my bosom and then a nice easy rubbing on my nature. It felt so mighty wonderful I knowed it was a dream, so I kept my eyes shut tight trying to hang on to a good feeling. Can you blame me, Lord? I'd had so many bad dreams. Pretty soon I was moving against that softness till I found relief. Behind my eyes was still a bunch of stars, so I counted em till all the lights went out.

"Way afterwhile I heard a whispering in my ear, then felt my hand being moved to a soft spot. 'Tom, do me. Do me now, it's my turn.'

"I heard her whispering like cool air through the trees. I swear to God, if He still listens, that Juliette had put my hand between her legs. She was lying on her back looking up at me, holding my hand on a spot as soft as goose feathers and melted down like butter. 'God help us,' I say, before loving her all over with my eyes closed, and I make out like it was a dream so we wouldn't go to hell.

"I'd had bad dreams since I was six. My eldest brother used me like a woman since then. The first time he did it to me it hurt and I tried not to move so I wouldn't wake up lil Juliette. I make out like I was having a bad dream, cause if it's a dream you wake up, daylight comes, and it's passed. Me and Juliette had good dreams together. The night me and Juliette start loving one another different, I make out we was dreaming. Before I could think, I was giving her a dream. She kept her eyes closed, and I loved her lil body that I knew better than my own, loved it like it was mine. I give her a bath with my kisses all round her face and neck and the lil bumps on her bosom and all over the soft spot between her legs."

Miss Tom stopped suddenly and was quiet as the fish sleeping in the river. The sun poured on us, and I could hear the birds singing and branches falling in the woods behind us. My line got a bite, but Miss Tom didn't even look up as I pulled a lil wiggling baby fish, bout as big as a sardine, outta the depths of the river. I unhooked the lil fish without Miss Tom even telling me and threw it back to its mama.

"Growing up in a four-room shack on the Mississippi River in a house with six men, I dreamed a lot. But after loving Juliette in that way, things was different. My brother didn't come to me no more. Juliette stopped that. She didn't make out like she was sleeping no more. When my brother come to make me dream, she would kick him, bite him, scratch him. So he just quit and pretty soon left Mississippi to find a job up North. Juliette was jealous in a vicious kinda way, but she had a good heart. She wouldn't let no boys come round to court me. Not that they was tearing down the door. But some old men who was widowers with children needed another hand on they farm and they'd come round looking me and Juliette over. She would put the dogs on em.

"For nine years we slept in the same bed loving one another like it was natural. Then Mama died of TB, and Uncle Reb and Aunt Taylee come to fetch Juliette. They said they only had room for her. Mr. Boone say me and the boys could stay on the land and work it.

"'You and the boys grown,' Aunt Taylee say to me. 'You can make it on your own. You nearbout a old maid. Hmph. At twenty-one years old you need to be married. If you fixed up some and shaved off that mustache you might look more like a girl.'

"Juliette's heart broke in two when I told her she had to go, but I promised I'd send for her. She cried all the way down the road. I cried late that night into a pillow filled with the smell of her.

"After the funeral, and after Juliette left, me and Booker T., my youngest brother, set out for New Orleans on a shrimp boat with everything we own wrapped in a piece of newspaper tied with string. I kept a lock of Juliette's hair in a lil bag with some roots in it round my neck and touched it when I wanted to dream.

"A week passed and the only job I could find was washing dishes in a whorehouse. Booker T. got a job working on the shrimp boats the second day we was there. We rented a lil room in back of a stable yard and took turns sleeping on the cot they call a bed. Other times we'd sleep in a old raggedy chair with the springs popping out.

"New Orleans was full of big, pretty houses and pretty mulatta women, though none could compare to Miss Juliette.

"Out of the blue one day, Booker T. say, 'Tom, I bet you down at the shrimp boats they don't know you from a man. Your lip hair and sideburns thicker than mine.'

"Don't you know they went for it? I got a job shrimping the very next day and I never went back to the whorehouse. Soon after that I got into a trade school for colored men, and me and Booker T. was living in a boardinghouse with separate rooms. He was feeling his nature and took to drinking and bringing women to his room. All I worked for was Juliette. All I thought bout was her sweet, pink smile, black cloud hair, and loving her soft white body till daybreak. I almost had the money to send for her when me and Booker T. got a letter that froze my blood. Uncle Reb and Aunt Taylee was sending Juliette to school up North. She had got a scholarship to a school in Canada, a teaching school. You could've knocked me down with a feather. Two years had passed already, the school was two more, and she was promised a job down South. I was crushed.

"I stayed lonesome for a lotta years, but fate led me to meet a woman like me. She was a real woman though. She liked to wear fancy dresses, put on bright jewelry, dash herself with loud perfume, and paint herself up—and she loved to dance. I was still doing mens' work, and even after hours we went out dancing with me dressed like a man. She named Ruth, but sometimes when we lay loving one another, I call her Juliette.

Most times Ruth be so drunk she never member what I call her or what we did. The only way I could love her was if I membered Juliette, my eyes shut tight counting stars and dreaming with her.

"It was twenty-two years before I heard from Juliette again. I got a letter in a handwriting that wasn't hers, begging me to come to her in Georgia, this very city, in the very house I live in this day. The letter said she was sick and wanted to see me one last time before she died. She begged me not to tell nobody else, I was the only one she wanted to see. The letter was signed, *I will always love you, your gentle sister, Juliette.*

"I packed everything I owned in a suitcase like I did when I left Mississippi and never looked back. I gave Ruth a lil piece of money and told her I was going to my sister and didn't know if I'd return. She cried some, and I hugged her one last time at the train station. But I never looked back on the bayou. All the way on the train I couldn't stop thinking bout Juliette. Sometimes I'd wake up and my face be wet from crying in my sleep. When I got to the address she wrote me she lived at, I got a surprise. It was a big, fine house for a colored woman, so I figured she might work there. Indeed, a white woman met me at the door. I had on a new gray suit and a stiff-brim hat. I stood there with my hat in my hand in a sweat.

"Scuse me m'am, I'm looking for Miss Juliette Perry. This address she sent me say she live here.

"The woman looked me up and down in a friendly sort of way, kinda curious.

" 'You Tom?' she finally ask me.

" 'Yes'm,' I answer polite as you please.

" 'I'm Lily. I been taking care of Juliette. She ain't well at all. I'm the one wrote to you. Why you dressed like that? You hiding from something?'

" 'No m'am. This the way I have to live to find work. Only work a colored woman can get where I been is cooking, cleaning, washing, or whoring, and I ain't partial to none of them.'

" 'You don't have to call me m'am.'

" 'Scuse me, but I just come from New Orleans and I'm used to calling white folks m'am.'

" 'I ain't white,' she say, smiling at me.

"You coulda bowled me over with a dime. She had them light-colored eyes, dark straight hair, and white, white skin. She was young, too. Couldn't have been more than twenty. She ask me to come in the house, took my hat and bag, and led me to the kitchen. She told me Juliette had been sick a month.

"When we was sitting at the kitchen table, she tell me what happen in them twenty-two years that was missing. She say Juliette moved to New York when she finished school and started passing for white. She was teaching school up there, and Lily was one of her students. Lily was passing too. They kinda helped one another out and was soon living together. Juliette wanted to teach in the South, teach colored children to read and figure, and she got Lily to come with her to study under a colored doctor to help heal coloreds. They was living here three years when Juliette was struck with this sickness.

"Then Lily showed her to me. My Juliette lay in a big iron bed, pale as a ghost, and delicate like a dried-up flower withering amongst all them quilts and plump pillows. I walk up to the bed and whisper her name real low. Her eyes open and shut like bird wings. When she see me, her eyes light up the black circles all round em.

"First thing she say is that she sorry for all these years gone. 'Tom, I knowed you'd look just like you do.' Then she just look at me, us not talking for a long time. Finally she say, 'You know I ain't got much time so I want you to come here closer to me and listen.'

"I did like she wanted. I sat on the bed close to her and took her cool, dry hand in mine and I heard Lily go out the room and close the door.

"Juliette sit up and speak stronger. She was still a beautiful, God's-gift creature. I tried to drink her up, swallow her up whole with remembering.

"'Tom, I wanna love you one last time before I go. I wanna love you with my eyes open. I learned how to do that with Lily and I want to give you something and take something of you before I go. And Tom, I want you to take care of Lily. She ain't got nothing, and nobody in this world to claim her but me. This my house. Now it belongst to the two of you. Promise me you'll do it Tom, promise me.'

"What could I do cept like always? 'Miss Juliette, I would die for you if I could,' I say.

"She squeezed my hand with a strength she didn't look to have.

"She didn't make love like a dying woman, but slow and natural like a woman in love, and I loved her back with everything in me till we was both wet with loving and empty of all but love. After she fell asleep I got up and washed myself. Then I bathed Juliette's body as if she was my sleeping chile.

"When I went out to the kitchen to get a pitcher of drinking water, Lily was slumped over the table crying her eyes out.

"'Why? Why you have to love her like that? Ain't she sinned enough with me? You her sister, and it just ain't right.'

"She wailed, like death was on her. She looked more like Juliette with every tear that drop. I hadn't noticed so much before how they had the same soft, black hair, white round face, and cat-colored eyes. Where Juliette was tall and lean, Lily was on the short side and kinda plump, but they could've passed for sisters and probably did when they was living up North like white women.

"'I love her as much as you do,' was all I could say.

"I put my arm round her and let her cry. That night I slept in the bed with Juliette, and Lily slept on the floor next to Juliette's side. We went on like that till Juliette died two weeks later, leaving us in mourning, loving her even into the grave. We kept loving her, too. After the funeral, me and Lily stayed up all night talking bout Miss Juliette. When it was time to turn the lights out, I took Miss Lily's hand and we went into Juliette's bedroom and lay down together. We been sleeping in the same bed every night ever since."

Miss Tom let out a cry so sharp I dropped my fishing pole and it slid in the river. I took her big, rough hand in mine and felt my throat tighten up and tears fall.

"Miss Juliette, I can't lose you twice. Lord, don't let her go . . . " Miss Tom said, with a grief deep in her heart.

We sat there crying on the banks of the Backbend River as the sun, a big red ball of fire, rested gently between the trees. Miss Tom seemed to come round afterwhile. She looked over at me.

"Lord, forgive me for what this chile have heard this evening, but you and me both know it's the truth. If you in heaven, God, please spare me losing Miss Juliette a second time."

With not another word, Miss Tom got up, dusted off the seat of her britches, and started gathering up our stuff. She took my hand and whistled a old blues song while we was walking home. Her telling me that story clicked the lock on our friendship and was never spoken of again, but that was the last time Miss Tom took me fishing. Like she predicted to Big Mama, my interests soon turned to other young folks, but I never forgot Miss Tom or her story.

Miss Lily eventually got over her fever and continued to heal coloreds in the community. She and Miss Tom probably still live in that big, old white house on Sixth Avenue, loving each other with they eyes wide open.

Maggie Agatha Christmas St. Clair

Better hold on to your money, the flim-flam man going round," Aunt Mae announced on Sunday night to her after-church drinking customers.

"I heard Henry got beat out of more than a hundred dollars down there by Kin Folks Corner. Alice is in a fit," Miss Corine said, putting a glass of gin and water to her lips.

Kin Folks Corner was a row of shops in the black part of downtown that faced the railroad tracks next to the river. Grocers on Kin Folks Corner sold fresh pork, hog headcheese, poke salad, skinned possum and rabbit, hand-churned butter, and all kinds of herbs for healing and root work. The combination hardware and feed store carried mule yokes and chicken feed. There was some clothes shops, a rib shack, liquor store, and barbershop.

A lot of folks that lived in the city come from the country. When they miss the country they would go to Kin Folks Corner for a piece of home. Folks from Prayerville and other country towns would go there Saturdays to buy the factory-made dresses, fancy handkerchiefs, hats and such on Broadway, the downtown shopping district's main street round the corner. Kin Folks Corner was a place where you was liable to meet somebody from way back in your past, your family, or get robbed by the flim-flam man.

As usual, I was sitting on a high stool in my corner by the refrigerator with a dixie cup of gingerale, pretending to be just one of the crowd. I'd heard of the flim-flam man, but I never saw one. Of course, I was never allowed to go to Kin Folks Corner.

"How he take somebody's money without a gun?" I wanted to know. All the grown folks I knew worked hard, long hours, and giving up a dime that was so hard to come by was beyond my mind.

They all laughed. Mr. Rogers, a big plum-black, bald-headed man with a gold tooth that had a real diamond stuck in it, was sitting next to me. He smiled up at me and said, "Baby, a slip of the lip has drowned many a ship. They got some characters so slick, they talk you outta your skin. They got some fast talking folks on the streets operating on the kindness of good-hearted peoples and the greed of most mens. Many times they make you think they some kin to you before they take off with your money and disappear."

Aunt Mae said, "Otis got took one time and all of y'all know he so tight he could squeeze fifty cents outta quarter. He say one of the fellers that took him was a nice-looking man wearing a suit, who in the course of they conversations said he was from North Carolina and knew some of Otis' people up there. Another colored feller dressed in overalls and a wore-out cap carrying a cardboard suitcase tied with a rope come up first. Otis said he talked funny, like he was a foreigner. Ask Otis to help him find a address. Otis got a good heart, he'd help the devil outta hell. So he commenced to look at this address and tell the man he never heard of the street. Otis see a policeman and suggest they ask him, but the feller say he don't trust white men.

"Then a feller a lil bit older than Otis come up. This one was wearing a suit. He ask what was going on. The young feller explained he was looking for this address he was sposed to lodge at. Then the foreign feller pull out a roll of money thick enough to choke a elephant and say he'll pay Otis twenty dollars to help him find this address. The feller in the suit say he can help, but Otis got that greed on him and say he got a few minutes and he feeling like he can use the twenty dollars for the crap game he was on his way to. The foreign feller then say he tired from traveling and he want a drink, so they start walking to a restaurant and on the way there the feller in the suit say he know where the foreign feller can get a drink, a bath, and a pretty girl.

"Well, don't you know the foreign feller's eyes light up and he like this idea, but he say he heard bout them kinda places and he start flashing that roll of money and telling them how he afraid they take his money in that place. The feller in the the suit suggest Otis hold the money till they get back. 'How I know I can trust you man?' the foreign feller ask Otis. The feller in the suit say they could all put they money in a handkerchief together. That way they know they can trust him. The foreign feller agree. Even say he'll give Otis another twenty dollars and buy him a steak dinner if he hold the money. That did it!

"Otis pull out the hundred dollars he was going to gamble with and put it in the handkerchief with the other money. The foreign feller tied it all up and showed Otis how to hold it under his coat, under his right arm so nobody can take it from him. That's when the switch was made. The two fellers got in a taxi and was pulling away from the curb before Otis thought to holler he'd meet them at Kin Folks Corner in a hour. He still waiting. He stood on that corner three hours before he walked home feeling lucky. He was mighty surprised to find a stack of cut-up newspaper and not a single dollar bill. He was too shame to call the police.

"Them mens was never to be seen round here no more and neither was Otis' money. I do believe that Otis would shoot to kill at the sight of them thieves. And you know it ain't no use going to jail on no humbug. Two wrongs do not make a right, no way you look at it."

Everybody said a *amen* to that, took a drink, and soon start talking bout something else. When I got home that night, I ask Big Mama how somebody take your money without a gun.

Big Mama say, "What Mae and them drinking fools been telling you, chile?"

"Aunt Mae say the flim-flam man going round and that he take your money without a gun."

"Oooh chile, you don't say they going round again!" Big Mama shook her head and let her eyes look to the picture of Jesus on the wall. She kept on making up biscuits while telling me bout the flim-flam man.

"I have seen the flim-flammers with my own natural eyes and I have seen greed and love of money ruin many a mens and women. I was coming home one evening and a flim-flammer was on the back of the bus. It musta been on a payday, the first of the month I believe it was, or a Friday. Thems popular days with everybody. All the noise they was making caused my head to ache, but wasn't nowhere else to sit but on one of them long seats at the far back, sitting sideways.

"They was back there climbing over each other with greed. I saw this with my very own eyes. Two young mens beat twelve hard-working individuals out of most every penny of they paychecks. From downtown to the projects and back, I rode the bus twice just to see if they was to continue in they madness. Two fellers was working together. The first one was black as the ace of spades. He had a cut over his eye, and the teeth in his head that wasn't brown was black. He had on some dark glasses, probably to hide his doped-up eyes. He was back there playing three-card molly, Jesus."

"What's three-card molly, Big Mama?"

"If you hold on I'm fixing to tell you. It's a con game played with three cards—two red and a black or the other way round. The feller shuffles them round, and the fool is sposed to guess what card is odd and bet money he know. But these flim-flammers is quick with they hands, and you win if they want you to win. The first one had got up enough interest by the time the second feller get on the bus. This second one was high yeller. He looked kinda dumb with his hair all conked back and he had a mouth full of crooked teeth. He got excited bout the game and play some, winning two or three times what look like forty or fifty dollars. Then the others round start to play and course they lose hard. I don't know why in the name of Christ folks think they can get something for nothing." Big Mama shook her head again and pondered on that idea while she put the pan of biscuits in the oven.

"Folks just greedy is all I can figure."

Wasn't long after Big Mama told me that story that she come

home with a woman I ain't never seen before. The woman was walking behind Big Mama carrying two heavy-looking grocery sacks. She was kinda on the plump side and even with all them packages, she walked slow and sexy. Look like she smelling roses and time wasn't in her way. Her skin was brown as pecan shells, soft and smooth looking. Her hair was real long and thick and shiny. She had a habit of flipping it over her shoulder every few minutes with a quick motion in her neck. She was pretty, but she had on enough make-up to make a grizzly bear look good. The navy blue skirt suit she wore and the white blouse she had on under it look like they just come from the cleaners. Even her stockings matched her legs. But the black pointy-toed pumps look like they would hurt. This strange woman come in the back door to the kitchen behind Big Mama and set the groceries on the table. She was smacking on some bubble gum.

"Lady, can I go now? I got things to do," she said in a funny accent, kinda proper like she was from up North, while she looked up at the ceiling. She stood there posed like in a magazine, brushing her suit with her hands.

"You ain't going nowhere madam till you take that chewing gum outta your mouth. You look like a cow chewing cud. Now sit down, you staying for dinner," Big Mama said, and started putting groceries in the cabinets and in the refrigerator.

"Lady . . . " the woman said, raising her voice in a whine like my Cousin DeeDee when she want something she cain't have.

Big Mama give her a look sharp enough to slice a brick. The woman sit down in a chair at the table, crossed her legs at the knee and swung her foot, and looked at something on the floor by the stove.

"Who she is Big Mama? What her name?" I ask real shy, standing half behind Big Mama looking at the strange woman.

"Ask her yourself. She dumb, but she ain't deaf," Big Mama say.

"My name is Maggie Agatha Christmas St. Clair, and I graduated high school and had some college thank you, so I ain't dumb," she snapped, looking up from that spot on the floor by the stove.

"I ain't said nothing bout book learning gal. You ain't got no common sense and no conscience neither. Down there on Kin

Folks Corner trying to beat a old woman outta her money. You ought to be shame of yourself. They teach you that in college?" Big Mama stared her down. That shut her up for a minute. Big Mama kept stacking tin cans in the pantry and putting eggs in the refrigerator.

Maggie picked at the edge of the tablecloth with her long painted fingernails.

"I was tired of making a living on my back," Maggie said, her eyes on the floor.

"On your back?" I repeat, eyes wide, not understanding exactly.

Big Mama held on to the sink looking back at Maggie with a sick and surprised look on her face.

"Hush chile," she say, staring at Maggie like she from the moon. "You don't mean . . . "

"I mean I was a whore, a slut, a common streetwalker, a prostitute." Maggie stood up and took two steps to the kitchen window where Big Mama kept green plants and African violets. She felt the leaves between her fingers.

"You know that song, 'Nobody Knows the Trouble I Seen'? Story of my life. The colored orphan-home ladies found me on they doorstep on a cold Christmas morning in 1943. Ain't nobody never wanted me for Maggie. They either want something from me, or they took it without asking. At least with the flim-flam I'm working for myself. I'm tired of running, though."

She sound just like a lil girl, like DeeDee bout to cry. Big Mama took a step toward her, and Maggie fell into her arms and cried like a baby. I held on to Big Mama, and we all cried for a while.

Big Mama sent me upstairs with Maggie to show her where the bathroom was so she could wash up before dinner. As we was going up the steps Big Mama hollered up, "We poor folks, and I know each piece of jewelry I got, so wash the honey off your hands."

Maggie smiled a lil to herself. She took my hand in her soft plump one and started calling me Lil Sister.

"Lil Sister, you got pretty eyes. Can you wink your eyes?"

"No, but I can wiggle my ears," I say, showing her on the spot.

"I'm gonna teach you how to wink, Lil Sister. With eyes pretty as yours it'll come in handy," she said, smiling.

I led her into me and Big Mama's room, where we sat on the bed in front of the vanity with three mirrors.

"You gonna stay with us now?" I ask her.

"Depends, Lil Sister," she say, kicking her shoes off, "on the way the wind blow in the morning."

"I like you. You pretty," I say, looking close at the gold buttons on her jacket.

"I think we gonna be friends," she say, touching her hand to my face real light.

I sat on the bed watching her primp in front of the mirrors.

"You really do that with men for money?" I ask, leaning on the bedpost.

"I made some mistakes I hope you never have to. I wasn't a bad girl, but I felt like nobody wanted me and mens make out like they love me, so I went with em and fell in the mud. It ain't no kind of life. None at all. I was hungry for somebody to love me. I got two babies somewhere."

She flipped her long, shiny hair over her shoulder and brushed it hard with Big Mama's hair brush. I was surprised when she lifted all that hair off her head. Her real hair was plait up in thick cornrows. After all the make-up and fake fingernails come off she looked kinda like a ordinary person.

"You can be my mama if you want to."

"Where your mama?"

"She gone up North. It's been a long time since I seen her."

"What bout that lady in the kitchen?"

"She a old lady. Mama's sposed to be young. Anyhow, she cain't dance. If my mama was here she'd show me how."

"I'll show you, Lil Sister. I'm gonna show you how to dance."

And she did. She took a small transistor radio out of her pocketbook. Aretha was singing 'Rock Steady Baby,' and we did. We danced the Hound Dog and the Jerk. She even showed me how to do the Funky Four Corners and the Hula Hoop. We danced till suppertime. Big Mama had to call us twice.

That night Big Mama cooked a big supper—fried chicken, boiled corn on the cob, biscuits and gravy, and cold sweet potato pie. Maggie had three helpings of everything. She told us funny stories bout some of the tricks she pulled, the con games she played. Big Mama let it be known she didn't approve, but she had to laugh too at some of the crazy things greed could make a person do.

Maggie Agatha Christmas St. Clair got her big brown leather suitcase from the Greyhound bus station and slept on the sofa in our front room that whole summer. Every night she sprayed the room with a sweet, flowery perfume so she would have pleasant dreams. *Evening in Paris.* She sprayed some on a hand-kerchief I kept under my pillow, too. Maggie got so familiar, I could hardly remember her not being there. She helped round the house, did some of the cooking, taught me things in secret like how to wink my eye, wear make-up, and she let me wear her hair. She even went with me and Big Mama to church.

One Sunday Maggie got saved. During the call to sinners she walked that slow, sexy, smelling-the-roses walk of hers right up to the preacher, looked him dead in the eye, and shouted, "Save me!" Then she leaned into Reverend Waters arms like a fallen angel. Her hair spread over his white robe like a fan. I could almost swear I saw Maggie wink at him.

After Maggie was saved, she say she feel like she need Christian counseling, so she requested private conferences with Reverend Waters every evening after dinner in his office at the church.

Reverend Waters was over fifty years old, and he was married to Madame Waters, head cook at the governor's mansion. According to Aunt Mae, he was the kind of handsome that give young women hot flashes and old ones weak knees. He was tall as a tree and had, I believed, eyes that could see a sinning, wicked heart. His voice was like God's, rolling like thunder. It always woke me up outta a deep sleep on Big Mama's lap during service. A lot of women requested evening conferences with Reverend Waters, so for his protection his wife assigned Deacon Perry to sit outside the conference chambers. Deacon Perry was the youngest deacon in the church. He was a grown man, but he looked like a boy. Big Mama say he got sense, he just a lil slow. He was thirty years old and still lived at home with his mama.

Soon after Maggie started going to private conference, she

started acting funny, staring out the window, plaiting and un-plaiting her natural hair, and looking way off deep in thoughts. One evening when supper was finished, just before school start-ed, she come in the kitchen where I was shining my new school shoes. She kiss me on both sides of my face like she say they do in France. Then she give me one of her gold bracelets and a pair of earrings she told me had real diamonds in them. She told me to mind Big Mama and remember her when I say my prayers at night. When I ask her where she going she say, "To conference, Lil Sister," like she always do. But Maggie never come back. She run off with Deacon Perry who come back a few weeks later broke and by hisself. Maggie sent us a letter from New Orleans round Thanksgiving.

Dear Big Mama, I feel like you the only one been kind like a mama to me and love me without asking for nothing in return. Please find it in your good heart to forgive the way I left, but I am looking for my babies to give them the mama I never had, to love them. Thank you for everything. You and Lil Sister taught me more than college ever did. Inside this letter is a lil some-thing for your troubles. Please tell Lil Sister I be praying she grow up to be a good woman like you. I be praying for you too, Big Mama. Love, Maggie.

A hundred dollar bill fell out of the letter. Big Mama give half to the church missionary fund and the other half to Deacon Per-ry's mama. Me and Big Mama was sad for a while. We missed Maggie, and we missed her humming in the morning and her sweet perfume clouds at night.

Uncle Buck Loves Jesus, Sometime

Uncle Buck was Big Mama's half brother on her daddy's side. He would come stay with me and Big Mama when he had a falling out with his woman, Miss Red. Sometime it be for a few days, sometime a month or more, depending on Miss Red's mood of forgiveness. Most times he bring his old, gray hound dog Sam. Sam so old all he do is sleep and wait for suppertime scraps from the table.

"That dog too lazy to live. It don't even bark to let you know a stranger in the yard," Big Mama would say.

Uncle Buck answer the same every time. "Sam been with me longer than any woman I care to member. And I got something in my fist for any stranger coming in this yard ain't got no business round here." Uncle Buck would keep on rocking in the rough, wooden rocking chair he brought on the back of his rusty blue pick-up truck, blowing smoke clouds out of his pipe.

I loved Uncle Buck. When he come to stay with us, I would slip outta Big Mama's bed to sneak downstairs before daybreak and sleep on the sofa with him. His body wasn't soft like Big Mama's, but balled up next to him I felt safe there too. When I'd crawl in with him he'd grumble in his sleep, but he'd always move over and make room for me. In the mornings when I woke up he'd be gone, but I could still smell the sweet smoke from his pipe, the sharp scent of night sweat, and see sprinkled all over his pillow, tight curls of black and gray hair.

Uncle Buck was tall, way over six feet, cause he had to nearly duck his head to get in the front door, and he was a big man. I thought he was handsome. So did Miss Red and a few other women neighbors that lived down the row. When he came to stay with us, women would visit Big Mama to borrow sugar and things, but they always ended up talking and laughing with Uncle Buck out on the front porch.

"Julia Mayberry, I seen you looking better," Uncle Buck would say, on sight of one of the ladies.

"Buck, I ain't never seen you looking much better and man, you look a mess. Red done put you out again?"

"That woman . . . sometimes . . . I believe she could make Christ cuss."

"Buck, don't be taking the Lord's name in vain," Big Mama would holler from the front room.

"I was mad enough to spit fire when that woman throwed out some of my tires and things. That just wasn't right."

"Probably some old rusty junk making a fire hazard," Big Mama put in, coming to stand at the screen door.

"They was still good, woman," he'd say back to Big Mama. "Now I done some crazy things in my life, but my mama didn't raise no fool. The Lord knows I ain't never hit a woman or a child, though I been known to make a few grown men cry. I made the mistake of drawing back my fist at Red. You know I ain't touch her, just drawed back. And do you know that woman put a knot on my head the size of a hen egg with the bottom of a frying pan? Who wouldn't leave? She'll be over here begging me to come back, but I got a trick for her this time. She gonna have to cool that temper of hers."

Big Mama clicked her tongue like she'd done heard it all before, and we had. When Uncle Buck got too pitiful, and this usually happened on a Sunday after a night of drinking at Aunt Mae's, he would put on the only suit he owned, a clean shirt, and his spit-shined brogan workboots. He and Sam would get in his truck and drive over to Miss Red's to beg her forgiveness with something like a box of candy or some perfume from Woolworth's. Uncle Buck would come back to Big Mama's the next evening all hugged up with Miss Red and load up his truck with his beat-up suitcase, rocking chair, and hound dog—till the next time.

Uncle Buck and Miss Red didn't live far from us. So even when he was living with Miss Red regular I'd still see him down on the corner. He and his buddies played checkers out in front of Mr. Ben's Barbershop in the summertime and inside the front window in bad weather. Coming up the street two blocks off you could hear the sharp slapping of wooden checker pieces against the square of plywood that was the playing board, slapping checkers and the loud, rough voices of old men challenging each other.

"Hit me!"

"Crown dat king cause he fixing to rule this here kingdom and wipe your shuffling butt off the map." Slap!

"I been whipping you since before you was born and you still ain't learned who the master is." Crack!

"I know who the master is. I shave his face every morning." Slap!

"Yeah, and you cut me this morning, don't let it happen no more." Crack!

Uncle Buck taught me some trick moves and made me a playing board out of cardboard. We used black electrical tape for squares and RC cola bottle tops painted red and black for playing pieces. Sometime he'd be real quiet when he'd play with me. Look like he be concentrating on saving the world from total destruction. Sometime, outta the blue, he'd give me lectures.

"There's some good mens, baby. You just hold on till the right one come along or live a good Christian life without one, and don't you bow down to none but Jesus. Let no man use you for a whipping dog. Happiness is too easy to have by yourself."

Or on religion. "Some folks go to church every Sunday wouldn't be caught without a Bible in they hand, a cross on they chest, or a amen on they tongue. But if Jesus was alive today, they would step over him lying in the streets. More hypocrites in the church than sinning outside. Got feelings for nothing but they-self and they possessions. Folks talk bout going to church and religion. I can pray under a tree in my backyard or sitting on my front porch. I ain't religious, baby, I just love Jesus, love him in my own way."

Uncle Buck had a hard life. He told me time and time again that being born a Black man in the South sometime seemed a curse to him.

"A Black man has seen misery in this country, especially in the South. I'm gonna tell you some things you better member. You think colored peoples free, don't you, baby? Don't let nobody fool you into thinking you can relax, there's a heap of colored folks still in chains. You know I was born in Alabama . . . raised on a farm, so I was used to hard work. I got a notion to git married when I was bout seventeen years old. Me and Hattie run off with enough money to last bout a week and enough love tween us to last two lifetimes.

"Two days out we found a preacher who'd marry us. On the third day we felt God was listening when we met up with a fella said the sawmill was hiring colored families in Pineapple, Alabama. took us a day and a half to get there, but the foreman at the lumberyard hired me on the spot. Said he had work for Hattie, too.

"We was bout the happiest creatures on God's green earth till we saw where we was expected to live. A lil wood shack in the midst of bout thirty others just like it. Not a pane of glass in the windows, the door was hanging off the hinges, and the bed was a pile of rags in a corner. Not a blade of grass in the yard, and the well was half a mile down the road. Hattie cried when she saw that shack. After we sit there awhile I go looking for the man that brung us, but ain't no way to tell nobody we wanna leave cause the white foremans leave after sundown. The white patrollers, security they say, done locked the gates. Soon enough we get the message what they was protecting.

"We decided that staying one night wouldn't do no harm. We made up our minds that first thing the next morning we was headed out. That night Hattie and me scrunched up in a corner together and held on to each other. A loud noise woke us up. There was a beating on the door before it was pushed open with the butt of a shotgun.

"Two white men was standing up in the door hollering for us

to get up. 'All the men on the truck in fifteen minutes, all the women on the yard.'

"Baby, I tell you I was mad as hell, but looking down the barrel of a shotgun with a white man behind it like to scared skin off me. It wasn't even daybreak, black as night out there. I didn't wanna leave Hattie in that place, but them shotguns didn't give me much choice. I kissed her and got on the truck with bout thirty or forty men, and we was took a few miles down the road to the lumberyard where we was expected to work. I ain't never worked that hard since. Round lunchtime they let us take a break, give us grits, stale bread, and coffee.

"The thing that let me know just how bad the situation was happened just before five in the evening. A colored man come running out of the part where they was using them big power saws with his arm hanging off. He fainted not five feet from where I was shoveling sawdust. A couple of white men come over and drug him off by his heels. Man next to me said they was taking him off to 'the field' where they shot workers who was hurt bad or was too sick to work. Man said if I hadn't figured it out, that was the only way I was gonna leave Pineapple.

"I ask him how he get in there. Said he was in jail for vagrancy—he was just passing through on his way to Florida to pick fruit like he do every season. A white man from the mill come and paid his fine, and he had to work fifteen hours a day to repay it. Said he was lucky not to have a family. Families was held as hostage for debt owed on food and lodging. Well, I knew right quick I had to find a way out of that place.

"When I got back to the lil shack Hattie was crying. Her hands was almost raw from scrubbing floors in some white woman's house in town where they had hired her out. We knelt down and prayed, prayed all night making promises to God if He got us outta the mess we was in. And He came through—halfway. We slaved on that place for six months before Hattie died of pneumonia. She was always weak. I escaped and run back to Georgia the day after that.

"Don't nothing last long but death. Don't get attached to nobody and nothing you bound to lose or grieve over, God is sure to disappoint you. He let me get outta that place where many had died trying to leave. So I believe, sometime. Sometime I love Jesus and sometime I think he hard of hearing."

"Uncle Buck?"

"Yeah, baby?"

"All white people like that?"

"No, darling. Some folks just born without a heart. Some ain't human. They come in all colors and all kinds."

"How come God don't kill people like that?"

"Anybody can kill a man, but you can't kill a evil. Takes time, takes prayer and standing up for what you believe in, even if it mean you die."

Watch The Spirit Move

The weeks I didn't go to Miss Corine's, I watched Aunt Vi at the kitchen sink filling a mop bucket with hot soapy water on Saturday mornings. She reached up on one of the high kitchen shelves and poured a few drops of clear liquid from a lil brown bottle into the water and sloshed it round with the mop head. The clear liquid was holy water Aunt Vi stole from the Catholic church. She was getting ready to clean her house like she did every new moon using the holy water to protect the house from evil.

Aunt Vi mystified me. Like Big Mama, she was a Christian woman. Yet she believed in roots and spirit work where she depended on ancestor spirits to advise, herb and root medicines to heal and protect, and dazzling candlelit rituals to make the spirit move.

"Aunt Vi, why you need protection. Don't God hear you when you pray?" I asked her one time.

"Yeah baby, He can hear me, but even God need a back-up," she said, and kept on mopping.

Aunt Vi lived down by the railroad tracks in a tumbledown house in the middle of the block. Her house was set apart by

the wooden picket fence with faded designs in all colors painted on every picket. A pile of rocks, painted white, sat on the
ground just left of the fence gate opening. Aunt Vi said they
were another kind of protection. A cow's tongue sewn together
with hot red cayenne pepper and tacks folded inside were buried under there to keep her name out of the mouths of gossips.

The yard wasn't very big, but on every inch except the brick
walkway, a herb plant or flower grew. Tall stalks of yellow sun-
flowers, purple morning glories and poppies, a corner of cooking herbs—mint, dill, basil, hot red and green pepper plants—and
a corner of raggedy weed-looking plants that Aunt Vi used in
her root work.

The house had once been painted a dark gray with white
trim, but then it looked black and sooty with gray trim. It leaned
to one side, like the wind had whispered in its windows. Five
wooden steps led up to the porch that stood off the ground
on stacks of bricks at each corner and all round the house. Me
and my Cousin DeeDee used to play under the cool shadows
of the house, peeking up through the floorboards and listening
in on Aunt Vi's rituals. Sometimes she would catch us and pour
cold water through the cracks over our heads.

A rusted horseshoe hung over the doorway. Two cane-bottom
rocking chairs sat on the porch to keep off too many visitors at
a time.

"Folks is what keep bad luck in your house. I try to keep em
out of my house and my business."

Aunt Vi's house was comfortable and full of things to admire,
look at, and touch. It always smelled like the herbs and flowers
she kept hanging on nails all over the kitchen to dry.

"When I was a lil girl we didn't have money to be buying all
them fancy and highly expensive doctor medicines. Root medicine work better anyhow. Root medicine older than dirt," Aunt
Vi would say.

The bedroom was my favorite place in her house. There was
a big iron bed with a mahogany chifferobe and vanity to match.
The vanity was a special place of honor. An altar was set up
there in front of the three angled mirrors, colored candles, trays
of ashes and herbs, incense, river rocks and sea shells, bones

from small animals, a small brass bell to call the spirits, and small dishes of fruit, food for the spirits when they came.

When Big Mama was working and Aunt Mae had company or a party going on, I would be sent to Aunt Vi's house. Sometimes Aunt Vi would take me with her to find ingredients for her root work. We'd go to East Winston cemetery for graveyard dirt and blackberries, or down by the river among the water snakes and prickly briar bushes for special plants like poke salad, which she used as a laxative.

This particular Saturday after Aunt Vi finished cleaning the house we went upstairs to her bedroom.

"I'll never forget it as long as I live, the day that led Franklin, my first husband, to go see Sister Cora Walker Saint for a reading," Aunt Vi said, kicking off her house shoes and curling up on her big iron bed with a cup of bay leaf tea. She shifted her weight on one elbow and leaned back into the soft feather pillows with her eyes closed. I lay facing her propped up on one elbow with a jelly glass of my own.

"It all started cause Franklin's favorite cousin Showboat was getting married. Frankie wanted to be sharp for the wedding. So months ahead of time he get a advance on his pay to buy a new suit. He was proud of that suit. Bought it at Shomburg's down on Broadway. It was a sharp thing, gray sharkskin with big padded shoulders and long skinny lapels. The pants was peglegs, and he got a blood red shirt and tie to wear with it. He even went down to the pawn shop and got hisself some pretty imitation pearl cufflinks. He looked good in that suit. I must admit he was a handsome man . . . not bad to wake up to in the morning. That Franklin was a good, hard-working man. He didn't go to church though, too superstitious to step on a crack in the sidewalk. Always did put his clothes on left side first. Left sock, left shoe, left leg first.

"After the wedding, Franklin kept his suit in the plastic bag it come in. It was hung up in the chifferobe which we had to leave in the hallway outside our bedroom cause it was too big to keep in the room. Seem like he was always taking it out to look at. Way over in the winter, when he heard that his uncle was at death's door, Franklin went to the chifferobe to take a look at it. He'd done bought a black shirt to wear with it to the funeral.

"At that time we was living in that big, old two-story house on South Street. Franklin's Cousin Loreen and her husband Brewster Mack was living with us cause they didn't have no place and Loreen was pregnant again. It was kinda nice having company during the day. Loreen the one learned me how to play cards and smoke with her fast self. She'd do my hair and sometime I'd look after her lil baby boy. Brewster worked a day job in a barbershop downtown shining shoes and sweeping up the floor. He was a quiet feller, kept to hisself mostly. Franklin worked in a garage fixing cars, and Brewster was always teasing him bout being a grease monkey. Anyhow, Franklin went to the chifferobe and found that his suit, shirt, tie, imitation pearl cufflinks, and his Stacy Adams was gone. That man let out a cry to raise the dead. Loreen and Brewster had done took the baby to the county fair, but I knowed it woulda scared them bad as me.

" 'Woman, where my suit?' he hollered.

"I was out on the front porch and I run in to find him standing in front of the chifferobe. He asked me again, and I told him I ain't been near his suit. The man almost cry. He looked over every inch of the closet and all our rooms. He was still looking when Loreen, Brewster, and the baby come in. Course they say they ain't seen it neither. This thing worried Franklin so. Bout three days later he come home with a paper put out on the street by them spiritual advisors.

"The paper say something like: *How many times you seen ads in newspapers, on flyers, and in folks front yard promising to tell your future, heal all wounds, and destroy your enemies? Rev. Sister Cora Walker Saint brings to you the answers to the mysteries of life. She seeks to help people who have been crossed, can't hold money, want luck, want their loved ones back, want to stop nature problems, get rid of strange sickness, or find something they have lost. If you are seeking a surefire way to gain financial aid. Peace, love, and prosperity in the home, you need to see this woman of God today! Be amazed at the results gotten by Rev. Sister Cora. Satisfaction guaranteed.* Then it give her route number in Zebulon, Georgia.

"At the time I wasn't a believer, so I bust out laughing when Franklin told me he was going down to see this woman to find out bout his suit. He find out something alright. After she took his five dollars she tell him he find all the things he missing under his own house in seven days time if he do everything to the letter that she tell him. He was to wring the neck of a rooster and sprinkle the blood on the front steps, light certain kinda candles, and rub confusion oil on his forehead to help him think clear and untangle the mystery. Didn't take long. Day four of all this oil and candle business Loreen and Brewster move down to Vidalia. Brewster say he got a job picking onions. I was sorry to see em go. I knowed it be lonesome and quiet with just the two of us.

"On the seventh day, Franklin was downtown looking for a new suit to wear to his uncle's funeral when he saw his Stacy Adams and pearl cufflinks in the window of a pawn shop. The suit, shirt, and tie had been sold the day before. Come to find out it was Brewster who'd done pawned them things. Just like Sister Cora said, it was found under the house, under a snake living in the house to be exact. Well, Franklin wasn't one to let sleeping dogs lie. He was hooked then. I begged him not to, but he went back to Sister Cora to try to get revenge on Brewster. She give him some more things to do—boil turtle eggs till they was black, burn something belong to Brewster, light more candles and more incense. Ten dollars was her fee that time. It work, too.

"First thing to happen, Loreen run off with a soldier and left Brewster with the three babies. Then he got beat up by the Klan, almost killed. Then he lost his job and come back to Princeton with them three children looking like a family of rag pickers. What could we do but take em in? They was blood, family. Brewster begged Franklin's forgiveness for taking his suit. Said he owed money to gangsters and they had threatened to kill him. Brewster had lost everything. We was taking care of him and the children cause he couldn't keep a job and was on the verge of losing his mind, when Franklin realize he'd gone too far. It was all coming back on him: evil don't get nothing but evil.

"The third time Franklin went to Sister Cora, she charged him fifteen dollars to reverse the spell on Brewster, and for free she give him a lesson on the principles of root work. The main one being that by putting bad luck on a person, a negative, it was bound to come back full circle. In other words, you get out what you put in. After that Franklin never asked for nothing more than good luck and good health. Brewster finally got another job and another woman and went on with his life. Lord, that Sister Cora sure could make the spirit move."

They Tell Me...Now I Know

When I was a lil girl I knew the day was coming when I would join the circle of women. I knew cause Big Mama told me, and so did Aunt Mae every time I asked bout the lives of grown folks, or the sounds I heard behind late-night doors. Love, sex, and money. Grown folks' business. I waited for the day with the same longing as birthdays and Christmas because presents were promised as well as secrets and answers to questions only a grown-up could know. I knew the day I became a woman would be marked by blood.

The summer I turned twelve I got my first sign. Soon all the women in the community knew. Big Mama announced it at a regular meeting of the #2 Mission Prayer Circle as new business.

"Daughter got her blood this morning!" I heard Big Mama say. "We gonna have to take her to the river."

"I could've told you that. I seen the signs, I had the dream," Miss Mary put in.

"Look like time done sneaked up on us. She's becoming a woman. We gotta keep a sharp eye on her," Aunt Mae winked at Miss Corine. "The boys'll be sniffing round her like hound dogs afterwhile."

"By the time her mama come to us she was already on the road to ruin. It was too late to take her to the river . . ."

"Too late to take her anywhere. She was too fast . . ."

"And too pretty. Somebody had done already whispered something in her ear. She come in the door dancing."

"Left dancing, too. She left this world dreaming just like she come in."

"We can give Daughter what we couldn't give her mama."

"Daughter been restless, asking lotta questions."

"Bout time she got some answers."

"Her gifts, too."

"Yeah, we can give her what we couldn't give Fannie Mae."

After the meeting broke up I was called into the room and all the women hugged me good-night. I went upstairs to get ready for bed. Big Mama stayed up to wash the tea glasses and serving plates and read some from her Bible. Suddenly I was scared. They had mentioned the river. Snakes, prickly briars, and drowning. I had so many questions, thoughts, and feelings. I was still wide awake when Big Mama walked softly into the bedroom. I watched her undress in the dark and pull her worn flannel night-gown over her head.

"Big Mama?"

"I didn't mean to wake you up, baby."

"I couldn't go to sleep, Big Mama. When y'all gonna take me to the river?"

"On your birthday. We got all summer long to get you ready."

"Why I have to go now? I don't wanna go."

"Baby, your blood's come. There's some things you need to know and going to the river is a thing you need to do."

"It's a long way to the river."

She laughed, "Don't have to be no river there."

"Well, what happens at the river?"

"When a girlchile get her first blood her mama or one like her mama have to prepare her. Tell her things a woman needs to know. Then the women in the family can take her to a secret place for the crossing over."

Big Mama held my hand and started humming what sounded like one of Miss Lamama's African songs, whispering words I didn't understand. I felt comforted by the darkness. The song and the music drifted into my dreams of forests dripping with fine sprays of blood instead of rain.

I started spending more time alone with my Big Mamas. I kept hoping for presents like a camera, new clothes, or jewelry on my visits. Instead they gave me stories.

Aunt Mae's way of getting me ready was to explain human desires. "You feel like you wanna kiss somebody and hug em, that's alright. Nothing wrong with showing affection."

"What if they wanna have sex, Aunt Mae?"

"Now Daughter, you just twelve years old and I'm over sixty, so I've lived long enough to know sex ain't all it's made out to be. If you love somebody you can both wait till you ready to be responsible bout having sex. In the meantime you gonna have feelings, desire for being close to somebody. I'm gonna tell you like my mama told me. If it gets hot, fan it. If you cain't wait, stop long enough to make him wear a rubber. Look like we gonna have to make a trip to the health department and don't you tell sister, she'll just have a fit. You wanna hear bout the first time I made love with a man?"

"Yeah, Aunt Mae."

"Reverend Isaiah Masterson was his name. Oh, now he wasn't a reverend when I met him. The only thing holy bout Isaiah then was his name. That man was smooth as glass. Move me like Mahaila's singing, and he was sweet as Karo syrup. Met him at a house party on Cornbread Row. My girlfriend Peaches saw him first, but it was me he asked to dance. He took me round that dance floor like I was a mop. I was weak with desire and I didn't know exactly what it was. He blew in my ear, told me I was pretty, and sweet-talked me into one of the back bedrooms. I was out of my clothes so fast he must've thought I was a professional. I was twenty years old and still living at home with my mama. I'd been thinking bout it and listening to my girlfriends go on bout it and I knew he was the one.

"Especially when he asked me if I was using any protection. I hadn't even thought bout that. Then I got scared. The last thing I wanted was to get pregnant at that time. Well, fortunately, he was prepared. When I told him I was a virgin, he laughed so loud I thought somebody was gonna come in. He was gentle, such a sweet man. It hurt like the devil, and there was a lil blood.

"When he was finished that sweet man turned over and slept

like somebody hit him over the head. I knew that wasn't gonna do. I woke him up after awhile and told him he forgot something. I asked him wasn't I sposed to feel something. He look all embarrassed, then asked me what I wanted. I told him I didn't know, but he hadn't got to it yet. He laughed again like he did when I told him I was a virgin. Said I didn't sound like a virgin. I told him not to mistake me for a fool. Never had so much fun in my life after that. Now that was an experienced man, just a lil lazy. He ain't had but one rubber so he had to get real creative. Never met another man quite like him.

"But there's more to being together than making love, and Isaiah moved round too much. Here today gone tomorrow. Chile, don't get involved with a travelin man unless you wanna spend a lotta time looking out the window waiting for trains and crying.

Miss Mary, Miss Tom, Miss Lamama, and the other women told me bout some more things I'd need to know to get on in the white man's world, as they called it.

"Keep your own money—be independent."

"Treat other folks like you wanna be treated, but let no one walk over you. Stand up for yourself."

"Remember where you come from. You meet the same folks on the way up as you do on the way down."

"Pray. Put faith in the Lord and in yourself."

"If you don't want a baby, keep your legs crossed and your dress tail down."

"Let not your heart be troubled, the Lord is watching over you."

My thirteenth birthday was on a Saturday in late September. It was a beautiful, crisp day. Everything was clear, sharp. Downstairs Big Mama was cooking my favorite breakfast—pancakes, fried oysters, and meal-fried green tomatoes. A bunch of wild flowers and a basket of fruit were on the coffee table, with a pink birthday card signed by all my Big Mamas.

When night come, so did the women. Me, Big Mama, and Miss Corine got into Aunt Mae's big white fishtail Cadillac. The other women rode with Miss Lamama who was driving her husband's taxicab. We ended up at our church. Miss Lamama had a key since she was head of the Usher Board. It was strange being there with just the eight of us in the red-carpeted, softly lit room.

Big Mama took me into the pastor's study and dressed me in a snow white choir robe and tied my hair with a length of white gauzy material. She kissed me and led me back into the church where the other women had changed into different rainbow-colored robes. Miss Lamama wore yellow, Miss Corine wore pink, Miss Mary wore purple, Aunt Mae wore red, Big Mama put on a royal blue one, Aunt Vi wore a lavender one, and Miss Tom wore green. It was dark, and each woman carried a short, fat white candle that smelled of vanilla and a small bundle wrapped in white cloth. They gathered round me as we headed out the back door. In the quiet clearing between the tall pines I could smell the pine sap and feel the soft pine needles under my bare feet.

The women circled me and began to sing Miss Lamama's African song. *Yemenjah, Yemenjah. . . .* Miss Mary beat her drum and Miss Lamama shook her prized red-beaded calabash.

Big Mama entered the circle and faced me. She spoke first. "That your eyes may see truth and heart have faith in things you cannot see." She dipped her finger in a small wooden bowl and touched my forehead and chest with oil.

"That your arms and hands find productive work, that is helpful to your neighbor." Miss Mary touched my shoulders and hands with the oil which had been passed to her.

"That your feet carry you away and back to us when it is time." Miss Corine said.

"May you love with your heart and eyes wide open," Miss Tom said.

"Welcome Rita, never fear, we are with you always near. Close to the river, moon bleed through . . ."

"We will guide you, guide you through," all the women responded.

Each woman called me by my name as they gave my gift, hugging me, their tears mingling with mine. Big Mama gave me a small Bible with a white-beaded cover I knew had belonged to her mother. Miss Mary placed some of her special protection beads round my neck. Miss Corine laid a beautiful silk scarf over my head. Miss Lamama laid a length of heavy African cloth over my left shoulder and kissed me on both cheeks. Aunt Mae put a handful of five-dollar bills into a small change purse attached to a string and placed it round my neck. Aunt Vi sprayed me with my first perfume from a cut-glass atomizer bottle. Miss Tom gave me a book of poems by Langston Hughes.

I felt a cool breeze. It must've been the strong incense and the brightness of the candles that caused me to see my blood mama, Fannie Mae, standing behind the trees blowing me a kiss. She seemed to float away in my memory. These women were my mamas. They had always been there to give me whatever I thought I needed. Standing in that circle of light behind the Eighth Street Baptist Church on a clear September night I was given my name and invited into the circle of women, no longer a lil girl. I was a woman now. All the stories they had told me were gifts, all the love more precious than gold. They tell me . . . now I know.

Firebrand Books is an award-winning feminist and lesbian publishing house committed to producing quality work in a wide variety of genres by ethnically and racially diverse authors. Now in our fourteenth year, we have over ninety titles in print.

You can buy Firebrand titles at your bookstore, or order them directly from the publisher, 141 The Commons, Ithaca, New York 14850, (607) 272-0000.

A free catalog is available on request.

Visit us at our website at www.firebrandbooks.com